KV-389-344

LOVE'S DELUSION

Nan Pemberton

Curley Publishing, Inc.
South Yarmouth, Ma.

Library of Congress Cataloging-in-Publication Data

Pemberton, Nan.
   Love's delusion / Nan Pemberton.—(lg. print ed.)
      p.   cm.
   1. Large type books.   I. Title.
   [PS3566.E445L68   1990]
   813'.54—dc20
   ISBN 0–7927–0596–3   90–3623
   ISBN 0–7927–0597–1 (soft)   CIP

Copyright © 1980 by Nina Pykare

Published in Large Print by arrangement with Donald MacCampbell, Inc. in the United States, Canada, the U.K. and British Commonwealth and the rest of the world market.

Distributed in Great Britain, Ireland and the Commonwealth by CHIVERS LIBRARY SERVICES LIMITED, Bath BA1 3HB, England.

Printed in Great Britain

*For those
who believe in love
– and find it –
the ultimate reality*

LOVE'S DELUSION

Chapter 1

Miss Jocelyn Franklin adjusted the large Venetian straw bonnet that nestled on her dark curls and framed a heart-shaped face of enchanting beauty and firm countenance. As her closed carriage moved slowly along, she surveyed the London streets. It had been four years since her season, four years since she had seen the city's hustle and bustle. Her lips set in a stubborn line at the memory. How angry her father had been as she turned down suitor after suitor.

"I'm giving you only the one season," he had warned grimly. "And after that it's back to Sussex. I'll not pay any longer for such foolishness."

"That's quite all right, Papa," she had assured him. "If, during a whole season, I cannot find a man I can stand the thought of marrying, I shall not expect to find one at a later date."

Somehow this had not raised her father's spirits at all, and she really did not blame him. It must have been quite a trial for the poor man, finding his own stubbornness so well mirrored in his second daughter. But Jocelyn had held firmly to her resolve.

She did not tell her father, for she considered such niceties beyond his comprehension – a comprehension that saw only finances and blood – that she was looking for a man she could respect and love. Among the simpering beaux and exquisites that thronged to the theater and to the opera there were few she could respect, and not one she could love. Of course, at that time the Peninsular War had deprived society of its finest men, so her choice had been limited.

So Jocelyn had returned home to Sussex and resigned herself to the little-coveted condition of spinsterhood. Far better, she told herself firmly, to be the butt of stupid jokes than to endure a loveless marriage. The rude buffoons who scoffed at a poor woman's unmarried condition could at least be walked away from, but a husband whom one could not love was always there, demanding his rights.

Though the spring day was quite temperate, Jocelyn shivered inside her closed carriage. Nine years had not been sufficient time to wipe from her memory the sight of Maria's tear-stained face after she had been informed that she would marry Edward, Lord Mountcastle. It was not that Mountcastle was

2

a bad man or a rake, but he was more than thrice Maria's seventeen years, and she knew her sister felt no affection for him.

Thirteen-year-old Jocelyn had urged her sister to fight. "Papa can't *make* you marry anyone," she had reminded her sister. But Maria was too kind and gentle to employ the kind of stubbornness that had later saved – or doomed – Jocelyn. So Maria had gone to the altar, and now, nine years later, she was a widow with two sons to raise.

Jocelyn sighed. She was glad that she and Maria had been regular correspondents. Mountcastle could frank their letters, so they wrote as long and as often as they pleased. And, although Maria's letters had been unfailingly cheerful, it had not taken Jocelyn long to read between the lines.

Poor Maria was longing for something that Mountcastle, in spite of his devotion to her, had been unable to provide. She was longing for someone to love. Absently, Jocelyn toyed with her bonnet ribbon; perhaps she had been so adept at picking up her sister's longing because she herself was sometimes caught with a similar kind of desire. For the moment she dismissed that from her mind; her concern now was for Maria.

Now that her sister's period of mourning was over, she could begin to expect gentlemen callers, suitors who were quite willing to take over Mountcastle's wife and sons – and his fortune. It was this consideration that had brought Jocelyn out of seclusion in Sussex. This time she was going to see that Maria pleased herself in the choice of a husband, but she also wanted to be sure that her gentle, trusting sister was not deceived by some fortune hunter. Better to live alone, she meant to tell Maria, than to live without love and respect.

Jocelyn found that she was twisting her hands nervously in her lap. The prospect of Maria receiving suitors, of having a chance at a new life, had wreaked havoc with her own hard-earned acceptance, and she realized that some vital part of her own self still yearned for a man to love. Well, she told herself briskly, she was not determined to remain a spinster, and if by some miracle a likely man appeared, she would certainly not dismiss him out of hand.

Then she smiled at herself; such thoughts were really rather foolish. Even in Sussex suitors had not ceased calling, but not one had succeeded in changing her mind. Their chances had not been greatly improved by the knowledge that since her parents' death she was quite a wealthy woman and did not need a husband's support . . . wealthy in her

4

own right, too, with complete control of her funds. How foolish such men were to think she would be eager to put her fortune and her future in the hands of some simpering weakling like Mr. Ancton, or a bore old enough to be her father, like the pompous Sir Firley. And all for the so-called privilege of being a wife. No, indeed, she was no such fool.

But this thinking was a waste of time. She was in London on Maria's behalf, and that was the end of it. She stopped her musings and looked out her carriage window at the city. The streets were thronged with people, all seemingly going about on purposeful errands. She heard the cries of "Chairs to mend! Chairs to mend!" and saw the mender practically hidden under his burden of rushes.

"Baskets, baskets!" came another call from a pretty young gypsy, hardly more than a child, who smiled under her load.

Cries of "Bellows to mend!" came in one side of the carriage and "Mackerel! Mackerel!" in the other.

Jocelyn smiled to herself. She had always found the city a strange place – amusing, but strange. She had not become used to it in the year she had spent here – her "coming out" year. After her father's death

5

she had considered moving to London, but had decided against it. She had been loath to leave the old house in Sussex. She was comfortable there with her elderly aunt, an unobtrusive chaperone, and was accepted by the neighbors. She was used to doing as she thought best, and by now they were used to it, too, which was fortunate since Jocelyn had never been known to change to please others or to move from a position once she had decided to declare it.

"As stubborn as the old man," she knew the neighbors said when they talked about her, but she did not mind. Life was rather dull in Sussex, and her battles gave them something to talk about.

Jocelyn smiled. It was that very bulldog stubbornness that had endeared her to the "old man" – her father. He would never have left Maria's inheritance in her own hands. She was far too gentle and malleable to take care of herself in the sophisticated and worldly society of the *ton*.

It was stories of the social marriages, bartering titles for money, that had soured Jocelyn on the whole prospect of marriage. She felt it was quite possible that two relative strangers who married might learn to love – or at least respect – each other. But when the very foundation of their union was greed – what hope could be held for such a relationship?

No. She settled the bonnet more firmly on her head, unconsciously straightening her back. Such doings were not for her.

Absently, she fingered the ribbons that tied the bonnet. Undoubtedly this bonnet was greatly out of style; shapes and even colors changed drastically in only a few years. But she had felt the need for something cheerful when she set out for London, and so without much thought she had picked up the Venetian bonnet with its wreaths of straw and bobbing artificial flowers. She wished now that she had been more conservative in her choice. Her eyes scanned the streets for examples of the current modes, but it was still before noon – no fashionable ladies were about this early. They were probably all still abed, and besides, the coach was still far from the more exclusive areas which were the usual haunts of the *ton*.

Jocelyn frowned, her arched brows drawing together. Enough silliness about a bonnet; if it wasn't right, she would simply buy another. She meant to get some new gowns while she was in the city; just because she was twenty-two and unmarried did not mean that she had to dress as though she had one foot in the grave. Some fashionable gowns would cheer her up, she thought; lately she had not been feeling as contented as usual. But she must stop thinking of herself; Maria would need cheering and encouragement. She needed to pay attention to her sister's life, not become sentimental about her own.

She looked toward the big box at her feet. It had been four years since she'd seen Maria's boys; Tom was now eight, and Harold was six. She wondered if they would remember their aunt. She felt sure they would like the gift she had brought them – two puppies from Cassie's last litter. They were two of the cutest pups imaginable. Whoever said bulldogs were ugly just did not look at them properly. And they were of excellent stock, their father, Challenger, never having been bested in a fight. She imagined how excited the boys would be. She only hoped they would not both want the same one; that happened so often with children. Looking back, she could remember many times when Maria had given in to her, the stubborn, though younger, sister.

Well, thought Jocelyn, there was no use borrowing trouble, and perhaps this tutor Maria had spoken of – Peter Ferris – would know how to handle such a situation should it arise.

She leaned back against the seat as the

carriage moved into the residential districts. Here the houses were larger and more impressive, obviously prized possessions. Jocelyn did not care much for fashion or possessions. The house in Sussex was old and unfashionable, a big barn of a place, but she loved it dearly. It was distinctive and had its own character, something that these newer houses could not hope to equal. As she recalled, she had not cared much for Maria's house on St. James's Square. It had been too ostentatious for her taste, and she wondered how Maria managed to live comfortably amid so much splendor. On reflection, though, Jocelyn supposed that one could learn to live with anything. Perhaps the luxury had been easier to bear than her union with Mountcastle.

It had been apparent that Mountcastle had cared for his young bride, and Jocelyn knew that Maria had been a good and faithful wife to him. She also knew indisputably that Maria longed for someone to truly love and share her life with. Exactly how she knew this, Jocelyn could not say. Perhaps it was because she sensed the same sort of longing deep within herself. In her case it was improbable that she would ever find someone to care for. It was not likely that she would ever meet a man who could best her in an argument, and he certainly had to do at least that to gain her respect.

No, all those sentiments about love and passion that handsome young poets like Lord Byron were fond of running on about – those things, if they existed at all, were for gentle females like Maria, women who could use the guidance of a good man. Jocelyn sighed. She had never met a man with an understanding to equal her own, and by now she was quite sure she would not. Still, she thought, a smile curving her lips, there was certainly no harm in keeping an open mind.

She pulled thoughtfully at a black curl that had stolen from beneath her bonnet which failed to control the unruliness of her dark curls, but was not unbecoming. Jocelyn herself was unaware of her beauty, regarding all compliments as to the fairness of her skin, the texture of her hair, or the brightness of her blue eyes with suspicion born of the knowledge that most men married for money, and her inheritance was considerable. Her twenty-two years sat easily on her, and in spite of the outmoded bonnet, no one seeing her would have assumed her to be anything but Quality.

She stroked one of the velvet squabs. This carriage, with its red velvet upholstery, had been one of her first – and few – extravagances when she had come into her father's money. But the cushions had worn quite well. She really had not thrown her money about or been impulsive; instead, she had learned how to manage it herself. She did not depend upon her steward, for she enjoyed the management of her estate and did not like to trust someone else with her inheritance. She knew to a tuppence where and how her investments were placed.

Jocelyn did not deny that it was pleasant to have money, but sometimes when suitors came to call she was tempted to reconsider. She would rather not have to endure the admiration of those money-hungry aristocrats. She supposed it was not really dishonest for men to choose a wife by the plumpness of her pocket, but she did think they might at least be straightforward about it instead of expecting a woman to swallow a host of empty compliments about skin like lilies and lips like roses.

The trouble with money was that its possessor must always be unsure. Was it herself or her money that had prompted a man's offer? And she could never know – not for certain. Jocelyn leaned back against the cushions and sighed. She had determined on this trip to London to keep Maria from such pitfalls. Of course, she had not told Maria

11

the real reason for this visit, but she meant to keep her eyes open, and woe to anyone who attempted to hurt her beloved sister.

Momentarily Jocelyn wondered about the Viscount Ashburton. As Mountcastle's sister's son, Ashburton had been appointed Maria's guardian. Jocelyn had never met the man, and she hoped to keep it that way. Something in Maria's letters indicated that her sweet-natured sister had found him distressing.

It was unfortunate that he had to be Maria's guardian. Level-headed as she was, Jocelyn had to admit that Maria needed a financial guardian. But, she told herself, Maria needed such a guardian precisely because society had never allowed her to learn how to manage for herself. If it had, she would be perfectly competent to manage her own affairs and those of her sons.

Jocelyn supposed that Mountcastle, who had not cared much for gaming, had left Maria well provided for. Money would not be a problem, except that it would attract fortune hunters. Jocelyn smiled grimly. She had had ample experience in dealing with their ilk. She could see through one at first glance.

The carriage slowed perceptibly and Jocelyn looked out the window. The *ton* might think St. James's Square was a good place to live, but she did not. Her Sussex sensibilities were offended by the rows of great town houses, their walls abutting each other, reaching up into the sky. A house was meant to sprawl out over a great piece of ground, not to be squeezed and distorted into these pinched-up caricatures that had to be four and five stories high. It was true that land in suburbs like this one was expensive, yet the idea of a great house only two rooms wide struck her as ludicrous.

As the carriage passed slowly on, she let her eyes travel over the houses. The brick was all right – brick always looked substantial – and the iron work was of superb quality. Her father had once taken an interest in the making of ironwork fences, railings, and balconies, and she had found, somewhat to her surprise, that she shared his interest. She knew immediately that this was work of fine quality. The houses were handsome enough, all things considered.

The carriage drew to a halt and Jocelyn looked at the house where she expected to spend the next few months. It looked very much like its neighbors. After spending so much money, thought Jocelyn rather uncharitably, one should at least get a little variety. Then Smithers was opening the carriage door and she let him help her down. The front door of the house opened, too, and Maria came hurrying down the walk toward her.

Chapter 2

"Jocelyn! Oh, Jocelyn!" Maria's gentle round face was radiant as she clasped her sister in her arms. "It's so good of you to come. I have missed you so."

"I have missed you, too," replied Jocelyn after the hug, her eyes swiftly taking in her sister's appearance. Maria looked well. Her pale blonde hair gleamed in the sunlight and she looked happy.

"Come, come. The boys are in the schoolroom. They are anxious to see you."

This reminded Jocelyn of her gift. "Smithers, take the carriage around to the stables and then see that the box is brought in."

Smithers' homely face broke into a grin. "Yes, Miss." Cassie's pups were famed in the whole shire, and these two boys were getting the pick of the litter.

Maria took her sister's hand. "We just took down the mourning yesterday. The house almost looks strange without it."

14

"I would have come sooner," Jocelyn began.

"I know, my dear. But it was really better not to. Mourning is a dreadful business, and you had just finished with Papa's."

"But, still," said Jocelyn, "I would have been glad to keep you company."

Maria smiled at her sister. "I thought you were better off in Sussex with Aunt Beatrice." She sighed, the smile vanishing. "But now that the mourning is over and Ashburton says I must prepare to receive callers . . . well, I shall be very glad for your support."

"Ashburton says you *must* receive callers?" repeated Jocelyn as they climbed the front stairs.

Maria sighed again. "Well, at least that's the impression he gave me. He said I am too young to remain a widow."

"I can agree with that," said Jocelyn, who looked at her sister with a smile.

Maria did not return it. "Yes, perhaps. But Ashburton has such a way about him. It – it makes me uncomfortable."

"How?" asked Jocelyn curiously.

"He is so – so intimidating." Maria shivered. "He glares at me out of his dark eyes and then he pronounces. He never *suggests* – anything. And he never, never smiles. He just tells me what to do."

Jocelyn grimaced. "I collect that he, too, is going to arrive soon."

"Yes, indeed. That's one reason I'm so glad to have you here. Even Papa did not frighten me quite so much when you were close."

They paused for a moment in the front hall before continuing upstairs. Jocelyn remained silent. She knew that at this late date there was little point in telling her sister that the more you gave in to men, the more they expected you to. But the Viscount Ashburton might well be surprised to find that she was not of the same gentle stuff as her sister.

What men like Ashburton needed was to have a woman stand up to them. She had to admit, however, that most women were not in a very good position from which to fight. Generally, the law gave men all the advantages. Even in her own case, it was probably just as much the fact that she had no near male relatives as the fact that Papa had admired her independence that had persuaded him to leave her funds in her own hands.

Yes, thought Jocelyn with a tight smile and a militant sparkle in her eyes, the Viscount Ashburton was in for a surprise. He had black eyes – probably little and piggy, she thought, building a mental picture of an immense, pompous man with a belly that strained his waistcoat. In her experience, such men almost always behaved as though they were God Himself. They inevitably felt they knew exactly what was best for a woman. That that "best" usually meant being married off with no thought to a woman's feelings, but a deal of thought to the money arrangements, did not seem to bother them.

Well, Jocelyn told herself as Maria chattered on about the boys and their doings, there was going to be no loveless marriage this time.

"Jocelyn!" Maria's tone was softly accusing as they entered a somewhat somber bedroom. "You haven't been listening!"

Jocelyn squeezed her sister's hand. "You're right, my dear. I don't deny it. But I did hear you say that this is to be my room. Just let me lay aside my bonnet and gloves and then we'll see the boys." She did not miss the fleeting look that crossed her sister's face as she removed the bonnet. "I fear it is rather out of style."

"Well —" Maria hesitated, obviously unwilling to hurt her sister's feelings.

"Maria, you goose, it's a ghastly bonnet, and I know it. I shall get a new one directly, and some gowns, too. I must be able to ask for your opinion and get the truth. How else shall I avoid making a cake of myself?" she asked, lightly teasing.

17

Maria smiled in relief. "Oh, Jocelyn. You know that you have excellent taste. But the bonnet is a little – But come, the boys are waiting."

Jocelyn laid her gloves beside the offending bonnet and followed Maria out the door. "I wonder that they have not been at us long before now."

"Oh, Peter – Mr. Ferris – would not allow that. They are waiting in the schoolroom, as they should."

Jocelyn, who remembered the boys as young scamps, eternally into mischief, could only shake her head at this. "I have brought them each a pup," she said, "of Cassie's latest litter, by Challenger. I hope it is all right."

"Of course it is. How good of you. They will be so pleased." Maria pushed open the schoolroom door. At the table sat two children. They gave every appearance of calmness except for their dancing eyes. Then suddenly they rose and rushed toward Jocelyn and she was enveloped in two pairs of young arms. "Oh, Aunt Jocelyn!" cried Tom. "How good it is to see you!"

"And you, too," replied Jocelyn, returning the hugs.

Tom turned apologetically toward the tutor. "I am sorry, sir. I'm afraid I rather forgot my manners for a moment." Catching Jocelyn's

18

look of surprise, he went on to explain. "I am the Marquess now and Mr. Ferris says I must learn to act like one."

Jocelyn nodded. "Of course. But does that mean you cannot show affection?"

Mr. Ferris smiled and moved to stand beside Tom, laying a friendly hand on the boy's shoulder. "Of course it doesn't mean that. There are times when it is perfectly proper to do as you feel like doing – and other times when it is not."

Tom considered this. "I think I understand, sir. You mean, it is all right to hug Aunt Jocelyn here in private. But in public it might not be?"

Mr. Ferris smiled. "That is it, Tom. A man must consider the moment and the fitness of things."

"I understand, sir."

"Well," said Jocelyn, looking from one boy to the other, "what have you two rascals been up to?"

"We're not rascals anymore, Aunt," said Harold gravely. "We are learning to be gentlemen."

"I see. And is it fun?"

Tom's puzzled look almost made her laugh aloud. "I suppose not, Aunt, but it is necessary. Mr. Ferris says we must be prepared to take our places in society and fulfill our responsibilities," he declared, with a gravity of demeanor that was touching.

"Oh." Jocelyn found herself without words. What sort of man had transformed her two mischievous rascals into these boys who were willing to learn about responsibility?

Maria took Jocelyn by the arm and led her across the room. "This is Pe— Mr. Ferris. Hasn't he done wonders with the boys?"

"I should say he has," declared Jocelyn. She found herself looking into a pair of warm blue eyes.

"Miss Franklin."

"Mr. Ferris." With a slight qualm, Jocelyn thought of the box and its contents. Would Mr. Ferris approve of such gifts?

There was a tap on the door and a footman appeared. "Miss Franklin's coachman says this box was to be brought to her."

"Yes, Ketter. Set it there."

Hearing the sounds of squealing and scrabbling that were coming from the box, the boys looked at each other in anticipation.

"I have brought you something," Jocelyn said, "something from Sussex. Open the box."

Both Tom and Harold looked questioningly at the tutor and waited for his nod before they fell to their knees and began undoing the string.

20

There was a moment's silence as they lifted the lid, and then Harold squealed, "Oh, Aunt Jocelyn, they're beautiful!"

Tom turned to smile at her. "They're capital, Aunt. Just capital."

"Look, Tom," cried Harold. "Look at that one with the black eye."

"Yes." His brother nodded. "Which one do you want?"

"I like that one, Tom – the one I showed you. Which one do you like?"

There was obvious relief in the older boy's voice as he answered. "That's good, Harold. I like the other one."

Jocelyn, casting the tutor a look of surprise, found him smiling quietly. She turned to Tom and asked, "Tom, if Harold had wanted the pup that you did, would you have given it up?"

"Of course." The boy looked surprised.

"But why? *You* are the Marquess."

"But that's why, Aunt. Since I am the Marquess, I have responsibilities and cannot always do what I want. Besides," he said with a grin, "I wanted the other one, anyway."

"I see." Jocelyn was surprised that a child of his age could not only understand his responsibilities, but accept them. "Your father certainly did a good job teaching you your obligations," she said.

21

"Oh, it wasn't our father," declared Harold, reaching for his pup. "It was Mr. Ferris."

"Our father was very busy," Tom added quietly. "He had a seat in Parliament and that kept him away a lot."

"I'm sure he was very proud of you," replied Jocelyn. She moved closer to kneel beside the boys. "Come, tell me, what shall you call these two?"

Harold, who was cuddling his pup under his chin to the obvious delight of them both, said, "I think I'll call him Spot. That's a good name for a dog, isn't it, Aunt Jocelyn?" he inquired with sudden concern.

"A very good name," she agreed gravely. "And what shall you call yours, Tom?"

The older boy regarded her with a frown of concentration. "He's going to be very strong, I believe, so I'm going to call him Samson."

Jocelyn kept her face suitably grave. "That's an admirable name."

She rose and turned to her sister. "I'm glad that everything was settled so easily." She sighed a little. "I believe I'll just lie on my bed for a while before dinner. The ride was very tedious."

"Of course, of course." Maria's face reflected her concern. "How unkind of me not to have thought of it."

"Now, Maria, I am not *that* tired. Before I go I must say something to Mr. Ferris." A strange look crossed her sister's face, but Jocelyn could not interpret it. "Mr. Ferris, I must congratulate you. You have done a wonderful job."

The warm blue eyes smiled into Jocelyn's. "Thank you, Miss Franklin, but I have only done my job as I see it."

Jocelyn smiled wryly. "I rather expect that some lords would not see it quite the same way."

Her smile was returned. "You are certainly right in your expectation," he replied. "But I occasionally find someone who agrees with me."

Maria took her sister's hand. "Come. You and Mr. Ferris can discuss the proper education of young lords at a later time. Now you must rest."

"Of course." With a last smile at her nephews, engrossed in playing with their new friends, Jocelyn followed Maria out.

"Isn't he wonderful?" asked Maria as they made their way down the hall. "I mean, hasn't he done wonders for the boys?"

"Yes, indeed." Jocelyn answered automatically, her thoughts far away.

Maria left her at the door to the room that was to be hers and Jocelyn entered.

23

She removed her shoes and stretched out on the bed. It was good to relax a little. It was then that Maria's words came into focus in her mind. "Isn't he wonderful?" Maria had said.

Jocelyn sat bolt upright on the bed. Of course! How stupid she had been not to see it earlier. It had been written between the lines of Maria's letters. Maria was in love with Mr. Ferris! Slowly Jocelyn lay back on the bed. So, Maria had already found someone to love; no wonder she was afraid of Ashburton's arrival. The pompous Viscount was not likely to approve of a marriage between his young aunt, the Marchioness, and her sons' tutor!

Jocelyn found herself giggling at her imagined picture of the pomposity's chagrin, but her amusement was only momentary. The Viscount held Maria's pursestrings, and such men were apt to be vindictive if crossed. Of course, the fact that Maria loved the tutor did not mean that her feelings were reciprocated; perhaps Mr. Ferris was interested only in the boys. He certainly had done an excellent job with them.

Jocelyn's forehead creased into a furrow. Either way, there was going to be heartache. If Maria's partiality was not returned, she would be unhappy and unwilling to receive other suitors. If it was, then Jocelyn foresaw the kind of battle that she herself enjoyed, but that Maria had always dreaded and avoided. Perhaps, in this case, thought Jocelyn, Maria might learn to stand up for what she wanted. Mountcastle had left her fortune in the control of another, but her heart was now entirely her own to dispose of. Surely she would fight for that right.

Jocelyn closed her eyes and tried to recall the expression on Maria's face. There had been happiness at seeing her sister, but now that she thought more about it, she realized that Maria's face had held a certain radiance. Jocelyn's eyes flew open again. There was another question answered. Mr. Ferris did return Maria's partiality!

How very wise Maria had been, thought Jocelyn, not to have disclosed her secret. If she had written to her, Jocelyn would probably have come storming to London to oust this fortune-hunting charlatan, her mind already set on seeing him as such. But now that she had met Mr. Ferris and seen his effect on the children, she had to admit that she was on Maria's side.

Well, she mused as she drifted off to sleep, they had their work cut out for them, the three of them – that was a certainty; it would be no easy job to convince the Viscount that Maria meant to marry Mr. Ferris and no one else.

Chapter 3

When Jocelyn opened her eyes sometime later, it took her a moment to remember where she was. There was a tap on the door and she realized that it had been a similar tap, moments earlier, that had awakened her. "Come in," she called.

A maid opened the door and poked her head in with a timid smile. "My lady says perhaps you'd like to be up and about a little before dinner."

"Of course," replied Jocelyn. "Thank you." She sat up and swung her legs over the edge of the bed. Perhaps it would have been wiser to have brought Mrs. Spenser along. She would have been more comfortable with her own dresser in attendance, but Maria had assured Jocelyn that the house on St. James's Square was well staffed. Spenser's daughter had been about to give birth to her first child. Under those circumstances, Jocelyn had thought it more appropriate to leave Spenser behind in Sussex with Aunt Beatrice. Perhaps she should ask Maria about this maid. She seemed a pleasant creature.

Jocelyn made her way to the cheval glass

and surveyed herself in it. The woman she saw there was of medium stature. Her figure was slender, and her heart-shaped face, framed by dark unruly curls, showed a determined chin, a straight nose, and a full, soft mouth. The whole effect was one of beauty and though Jocelyn herself was unaware of it, more than one gentleman's offer of matrimony had been inspired by her beauty rather than her inheritance.

She glanced at herself cursorily and then turned away. Sleep had sobered her somewhat and she realized that perhaps she had been a little hasty in her appraisal of Mr. Ferris. He *could* be a fortune hunter; such men were professionals at deceiving their victims. But the philosophy that he had taught the boys to practice, as well as believe, did not seem to indicate that, nor did their feelings for him.

Absently, Jocelyn made her way to the wardrobe and reached for a gown of pale rose sarcenet. It had long narrow sleeves and an apron-front bodice from which the skirt fell, reaching the floor in front and forming a small train behind. It might not be the height of fashion, but it looked well on her and would do for dinner. She twisted her hair in a simple coil.

When Jocelyn came down the stairs sometime later, she found Maria waiting. "Jocelyn, I hope you are all rested."

"Of course." Maria looked lovely in a gown of dark green silk, her blonde hair piled high in a cluster of curls. Her eyes shone in the candlelight. She did not look like a widow just out of mourning, Jocelyn thought; she looked like a young woman in love.

"I hope you don't mind having dinner in the dining hall," Maria said. "It's rather a great place, but it is expected." Maria wrinkled her nose. "Being a Marchioness is not an easy life. People have all these expectations as to how one should behave."

Jocelyn laughed. "That applies to a great many people," she replied, "including me. But I just do as I please, anyway. You aren't going to let the Viscount browbeat you into marrying again, are you?" She looked at her intently.

"Of course not." Maria flushed. "But he does terrify me. He's so – so overbearing."

"The best way to deal with such a man is to hold firm."

Maria shivered. "You haven't met the Viscount yet, Jocelyn. He may be too much, even for you."

Jocelyn laughed again. "Nonsense, Maria. No one is too much for me."

28

Maria looked as though she doubted this, but then she just smiled. "Anyway, I am exceedingly glad that you are here."

She took Jocelyn's hand. "Come, dinner will be ready. Pe— Mr. Ferris dines with us." She did not look at her sister. "Fortunately, Mountcastle had settled that before..." – there was a pause – "...so the servants were used to it. Otherwise, I would have been constrained to eat alone all these months."

"I am glad you had company," said Jocelyn, careful to keep her voice neutral. She would not intrude on Maria's privacy. When her sister was ready to tell her about her partiality for the tutor, she would do so. Until then Jocelyn would bide her time and just watch.

As they neared the dining room, they were joined by Mr. Ferris. Jocelyn watched the joy light her sister's face as the tutor appeared. He smiled gravely at them both. "Good evening, milady. Good evening, Miss Franklin."

Maria's face was radiant as she replied, "Good evening, Mr. Ferris."

Carefully, Jocelyn controlled her own expression. It was obvious that Maria did not realize how she was giving herself away. Mr. Ferris, on the other hand, merely seemed to be friendly. Jocelyn bit her bottom lip. If the Viscount had been here, if he had seen that look on Maria's face . . . the whole thing would have been clearly apparent to him.

The dinner was elegantly served by footmen under the supervision of the butler, Rears. Jocelyn, observing everything, concluded that Mountcastle's servants were well trained. The service was excellent, and no footman indicated by the slightest expression that Mr. Ferris was not as much entitled to such service as she and the Marchioness.

As for Mr. Ferris, his manners were impeccable, and if his clothes had been more stylish, he could have passed anywhere as a gentleman of the *ton*. He must be the younger son of a good family. They were sometimes forced to take positions as tutors, but were seldom as well prepared for the task as Mr. Ferris. They seldom held such sound attitudes toward position and responsibility, thought Jocelyn.

She was determined not to let her initial liking for the man blind her to any faults he might have, but watch as she might, she could find nothing to criticize about Peter Ferris. His demeanor toward Maria was faultlessly respectful, and Jocelyn had not been sure until, looking up from her plate, she surprised the look of affection that passed between them, that he did care for Maria. Unobtrusively, she returned her eyes to her roast beef. In the face of such emotion she felt embarrassed.

They were well into their apricot tart and Jocelyn was reflecting on how Maria shone in Ferris' company, how his quiet wit seemed to draw her out and show her to advantage, when the door knocker was heard. Moments later a hesitant Rears reappeared to announce, "The Viscount Ashburton, milady."

"Oh," Maria said faintly.

Before her very eyes Jocelyn saw a laughing, confident woman transformed into a pale, trembling creature.

"Tell the Viscount we are at table," said Jocelyn calmly. "Ask him if he wishes to join us."

"Yes, Miss," replied Rears and Jocelyn thought she saw gratitude in the old retainer's eyes.

"Oh," whispered Maria. "I did not expect him till tomorrow. I thought we should have one more evening in peace."

Peter Ferris shook his head slightly and Maria turned to her sister. "Oh, Jocelyn, I know I'm weak, but the man terrifies me."

There was a sound from the doorway. "His lordship says he has already eaten. He will await you in the library."

Maria nodded. "Yes, of course. We – we will be there shortly."

"Yes, milady."

"Offer his lordship some brandy," suggested Jocelyn.

"Yes, Miss." This time she was sure she saw the gratitude.

Maria toyed with the rest of her apricot tart. "I – I have lost my appetite," she murmured.

"Nonsense," replied Jocelyn firmly. "Don't let him bother you like that. I assure you, Maria, I will not desert you under fire." When this did not work, she chuckled. "Come, Maria, he cannot be any worse than Papa was. And you know Papa could not best me."

Maria brightened slightly. "Yes, that's true. You always tried to help me."

She pushed her chair back from the table and cast the tutor a despairing look. "We – we'd best go and get it over with."

It was apparent that Peter Ferris was fighting a strong emotion within himself. Obviously he wanted to comfort Maria, and just as obviously he thought it unwise to do so in Jocelyn's presence.

"You are quite right," agreed Jocelyn, finishing her last bite of apricot tart and pushing back her chair.

With one last glance at the tutor, Maria followed her sister from the hall.

"Come," insisted Jocelyn. "Put back your shoulders and stick out your chin. Don't let him bully you."

"Yes, Jocelyn," whispered Maria, but she did not appear to be feeling very different.

Well, thought Jocelyn, they would see now how the pompous Ashburton liked having to deal with a woman who wouldn't be bullied.

"Milord," whispered Maria to the tall figure who stood with his back to them, gazing into the empty grate.

He was taller than she had imagined, Jocelyn thought, and then the figure turned and she was unable to keep back a gasp of surprise. This was no pomposity with a swollen belly and an equally swollen head. The Viscount was a youngish man, somewhere past thirty, she judged, tall and well formed. He scrutinized Maria, his dark eyes unfathomable.

While his attention was thus occupied, Jocelyn considered him. He was quite a good-looking man, she thought, with the lean look of the sportsman about him. She could easily envision him up on a horse, ready for a gallop. His coat of brown superfine fit smoothly over broad, well-muscled shoulders, and his kerseymore breeches and top boots clad long, lean legs. His head, covered with dark curly hair, sat on a strong neck, and

33

the jutting of his chin and the firm lines of his mouth bespoke a certain strength of character. Eyes, dark and somber, framed by disconcertingly long lashes, were set under heavy black eyebrows above an aristocratic nose.

"I trust my early arrival caused you no inconvenience," he said to Maria.

"No, no, of course not. You are always welcome," she faltered.

"Yes, of course," replied Ashburton dryly.

She could see why Maria dreaded those eyes, thought Jocelyn, as he turned to her. They were very intimidating. Jocelyn, however, did not bow her head meekly, as Maria had. She would not allow herself to falter before this arrogant man's gaze.

For long moments their eyes remained locked. Then the darkly handsome Viscount turned back to Maria. "You have a guest," he said in an excessively formal tone that seemed to mean more than it said.

"Yes, yes. Oh, I am sorry. This is my sister, Miss Jocelyn Franklin. She has come to me for a visit."

"I see." The piercing eyes fastened on her again and Jocelyn was conscious of a rising irritation with this top-lofty lord.

"I am pleased to meet you, milord," she said, aware that her irritation had been evident

34

in her voice despite her efforts to conceal it.

"I am pleased to meet you, Miss Franklin," replied the Viscount. He added with a sardonic lift of his brows: "I am sure that my greeting carries the same sincerity as yours."

He was sharp, thought Jocelyn. She imagined that he could give the cut direct with the best of them.

"Yes, milord," she murmured demurely while giving back look for look.

His lordship looked at her consideringly, but then shrugged his shoulders and turned back to Maria. Jocelyn was further annoyed to realize that she was offended at being thus dismissed.

"Marchioness," he began.

Jocelyn could almost see her sister shrivel. "Yes, milord?"

"I see by your gown that you have put off mourning."

"Yes, milord. It *was* time."

Maria seemed to be apologizing, and Jocelyn could feel herself bristling up. She moved suddenly to her sister's side. "Sit down, Maria. There is no need to stand." She longed to say that this was, after all, Maria's house, but she stopped herself.

Maria allowed her sister to settle her into a chair. The Viscount did not seem to notice. He continued to pace back and forth before the fireplace like some caged animal in the Zoological Gardens, thought Jocelyn as she calmly selected a chair for herself.

"You did receive my last letter?"

"Yes, milord. But I did not expect you until tomorrow. Not that it's any trouble," Maria hastened to add.

"I did not think it would be," replied his lordship, without a hint of apology.

What a top-lofty, conceited tyrant he was, Jocelyn thought, taking everything for granted in that condescending way – as though the whole world was run for his comfort, and his comfort alone.

"The room was aired today," Maria continued. "Everything is ready."

"Yes, of course. The mourning has been removed from the house?"

Maria nodded.

"Good. I will be here for some time. I want to see that everything is in order. And, as I indicated in my letter, you are still a reasonably young woman. You will expect to marry again."

Maria nodded dumbly and Jocelyn felt a terrible urge to throw something at this irritating man who had so little regard for her sister's feelings.

"I am here to see that you make a wise choice. There will be no lack of suitors. Many

36

men will be happy to replace my uncle. I intend that you should not be taken advantage of by any fortune hunters."

"Yes, milord."

If Maria said that once more, Jocelyn told herself angrily, she would scream, or perhaps throw something. The thought surprised her, since she was not, in spite of her eccentricities, a throwing kind of person. It was infuriating to see her gentle sister bullied around by this, this –

She took a deep breath. "Maria, my dear, why don't you go and see to his lordship's room? I'm sure you will want to be sure that everything is correct."

"Yes, yes, Jocelyn. If you'll excuse me, milord."

Fortunately, Maria did not wait for his lordship to make any comment, but went immediately from the room.

Jocelyn smiled to herself. Now Maria could seek out her Peter for a moment's comfort, and she would stay here and keep his arrogant lordship occupied.

"Do you come often to London?" inquired Jocelyn sweetly.

The Viscount eyed her. "Often enough."

"I see." He certainly could be a man of few words.

"Do *you* come often to London?" he

inquired, his eyes lingering on her gown. Suddenly she felt that it was sadly outdated.

"No, this is my first visit in four years, since I had my Season."

"Your father could not find you a suitable husband?" he inquired with a deceptively innocent air that didn't fool her.

Jocelyn felt herself bristling up. "On the contrary, milord. My father found many he thought suitable. It was *I* who found them lacking."

"I see."

How infuriatingly he could say those two simple words!

"And you do not regret your choice?"

"Indeed not," replied Jocelyn. "Why should I? I do not need a husband. I am quite capable of caring for myself."

The Viscount raised a quizzical eyebrow. "Indeed. That makes you a very unusual woman."

Jocelyn allowed herself a smile as she met his lordship's eyes. "I like to think so, milord," she replied.

A look of something rather like surprise flitted over his lordship's face and then he shrugged. "I find that I am somewhat fatigued. I believe I shall retire. No doubt we will meet often."

There was little cordiality in his voice

and Jocelyn suppressed a sudden giggle. He might have lacked the belly, but he had all the pomposity anyone could have imagined. "There is little way to avoid it, I suppose, since we will be living in the same house."

Again his lordship looked surprised. Jocelyn kept her face carefully neutral. Let the Viscount discover what it was like to face a woman with spirit. He was not at all used, as his startled expression had clearly betrayed, to being on the receiving end of an attack.

The Viscount bowed shortly. "I will bid you good night."

"Good night, milord." Jocelyn was tempted to add, "Sleep well," but she was sure that such a sentiment would be greeted with derision, and probably rightly so. She, who had always considered herself, in spite of her stubbornness, a rather gentle person, actually found herself wishing the haughty Viscount a restless and unpleasant night!

After he had left the room, moving with surprising grace, she stared for some moments into the fire. The Viscount Ashburton was going to be a hard nut to crack, harder than Papa had been, and he had been no easy job.

Men like Papa, older men with very fixed ideas of young women, could be foiled by a passive resistance, a method she had used successfully to rid herself of unwanted suitors.

Eventually, of course, she and Papa had come to cuffs more openly. But she had always kept her temper. She had not once let Papa make her angry. *He* had gotten angry. Sometimes he had gotten so angry that he could not speak.

That, thought Jocelyn, was not likely to be the case with the Viscount. She would have to watch her temper when she came to cuffs with him, as she inevitably would, for the Viscount was going to be a formidable enemy – one to test her mettle, she thought with a strange feeling of excitement. And, if she did not miss her guess, they would be at it very soon.

Chapter 4

When Jocelyn opened her eyes the next morning, her first thought was of the Viscount Ashburton, and it was not a pleasant one. She frowned. If only Maria had more steel in her backbone. Well, thought Jocelyn, pushing aside her unruly curls and casting a look of disgust at the heavily brocaded curtains that enclosed the great carved bed in which she had slept, she could not help it that Maria was such a gentle soul. She was just like their dear mother. She, too, had always bowed to their father's wishes.

Jocelyn sat up and pulled aside the curtains. For the first time she really considered the room. It had obviously been well done and at great expense, but she did not like it. Like everything in this house, it reflected Mountcastle's taste, not Maria's. The furnishings of the whole house were heavy and cumbersome, ponderously loaded with gold braid.

She herself preferred a more light and airy style – the Grecian. It was true that it was sometimes overdone. Great, heavy men were apt to look rather strange when seated on such delicate chairs, and a room could be too light and airy. But then, anything in excess should probably be avoided. She sighed. This room gave her a distinct feeling of oppression.

The sound of childish voices reached her ears and she made her way to the window and looked out. She saw that it opened onto a closed courtyard. On the paving stones below, Tom and Harold were playing with their pups. Their voices rose in cries of glee as they tumbled about.

Jocelyn wondered what Mr. Ferris would think of such activities. She was about to turn back into the room when a sudden movement to one side of the courtyard caught her eye. In a corner, near a bed of late summer flowers, stood Maria. She was watching her boys play, a smile on her face, and beside her stood Peter Ferris. He, too, seemed pleased at the enjoyment of the children.

Jocelyn, turning away, found herself smiling, too. It appeared that her estimation of Mr. Ferris was correct. It was always gratifying to have one's estimation of a person's character corroborated. It was too bad that the Viscount had not had the benefit of a tutor like Mr. Ferris. It might have greatly improved his disposition.

To her surprise Jocelyn found that she was scowling. How strange that she should be so upset by the Viscount. Many men had stood in her way during the last year since Papa had died, and none of them had caused her to lose her temper. Not once had she felt like screaming or throwing things, but now she did.

The truth of the matter was that she was unused to having so little control over events. Jocelyn sat down suddenly. She had a clear memory of what had occurred between herself and the Viscount on the previous night, and she had assuredly not demeaned herself by throwing something at him. Yet there was definitely in her mind a picture of herself hurling something at the cynical, smiling face of the Viscount Ashburton. She closed her eyes and concentrated. Yes, she recalled the scene clearly. She had hurled, oh, Lord! – a glass of wine at his lordship and he had not even flinched.

This was the end, Jocelyn thought angrily, quite beyond the bounds. She had dreamed of the Viscount Ashburton! He had made such an impression on her that her anger toward him had stayed with her through the night and influenced her dreams!

Jocelyn began to pace the room, her cheeks flushed. This would never do. She must learn to control her temper or the Viscount would best her. A person in contention must always stay well in control of her feelings. She had learned this lesson early and she had always profited by it. Well, she told herself, anger or no anger, she would win out against the arrogant Viscount.

Sometime later Jocelyn made her way down the stairs. She hoped that she would find something more substantial for breakfast than chocolate and a sweet bun. Her appetite was country-bred and she was used to a more filling repast in the morning. Her days in the country had been active ones.

Idly, she wondered how she would spend her days now. She hoped there would not be too many callers with their endless rounds of gossip; that was something she had always abhorred. It had seemed so infantile, sitting around discussing the scandalous doings of a bunch of silly women who had nothing better to do than pursue men and the activities of equally foolish men.

Jocelyn sighed. What a strange place the world had turned out to be, not at all the place described in the stories her mother had read to them as children. Those stories had been about a happy world, a world where good children got their rewards and princesses married the right princes and lived happily ever after.

But the world was not like that. It was a place where good children often did not get what they wanted, and princesses, as well as other young women, were married off for money and political considerations. Happily ever after had nothing to do with it. This was a world where people, especially women, had to fight, and fight hard, for what they wanted, and Maria did not know how to fight.

Jocelyn found a footman waiting patiently. "I should like some breakfast," she told him.

"Yes, Miss."

"Something substantial."

"Yes, Miss."

The footman left and returned in a few minutes. "Cook will have his lordship's breakfast ready soon. She has added some extra for you."

"Thank you," replied Jocelyn, wishing that her country appetite had not awakened her so early. She did not wish to meet his lordship so soon in the day. It was quite sufficient, she thought, that she must face him across the dinner table. She had not even considered that he might be about at this time of the morning. She had expected such a fashionable gentleman to keep town hours and stay abed till noon.

Jocelyn brought herself up short. There she was again, fanning her anger against the Viscount. It was true he was arrogant and high-in-the-instep, but many of the exquisites and beaux who had courted her had been just as arrogant and top-lofty, and they had excited her, not to anger, but to laughter. Perhaps that was the answer here. Perhaps she should endeavor to see the humor in this.

Well, she thought, she was spending entirely too much thought on the Viscount Ashburton. She would dismiss him from her mind and think instead of clothes. She certainly needed some new gowns. Her old ones, which until her arrival in London had seemed quite sufficient, now seemed so far out of style as to make her feel absolutely ancient. She would speak to Maria about visiting the dressmaker, perhaps even today. A sound behind her caused Jocelyn to whirl. The Viscount Ashburton was standing there, watching her.

"Good morning, milord." She smiled at him pleasantly. He was, after all, only a man.

'Good morning." Ashburton's tone was even but not cordial. "I should like to speak to you about a serious matter."

"Of course," she replied, trying to match his gravity, but failing. In fact, some imp of mischief within her urged her to parody his sober expression, but she managed not to heed it.

"I understand that you plan to stay in the city for some time," he said.

"Yes, I do," replied Jocelyn. "Maria needs company."

"The Marchioness will be rather busy," replied his lordship. "There will be callers."

Jocelyn nodded. "I will not interfere with that," she said with a bright smile. "But surely Maria's time will not be *entirely* taken up with calls. And perhaps she will want some advice in choosing."

She had hoped for an answering smile,

46

but Ashburton frowned, his heavy eyebrows drawing together over his straight nose. "I do not want this business to go on forever. I want to get this thing settled, have her properly married so that I can get back to Dover and my own affairs."

Jocelyn felt her sense of humor deserting her. The man was impossible. "I see," she replied coldly. "It is rather like selling a piece of property, is it not?"

Ashburton stared at her. "I fail to take your meaning," he said stiffly.

"My meaning should be clear," she answered. "You intend to dispose of my sister with no regard to her feelings at all." Jocelyn was growing angrier by the moment and she did not trouble to conceal it.

"You are quite mistaken," replied his lordship. "I have no legal authority to force your sister to wed, but for her sake, and for that of her sons, I believe the matter should be settled soon."

"And what of affection?" cried Jocelyn, quite forgetting all her resolutions about keeping her temper. "What of love – and respect?"

The Viscount's face darkened. "Love is a delusion, a chimera chased by fools, of little consideration in a matter such as this. And respect is to be given to those worthy of it –

not to some well-dressed young dandy."

"My sister is not a fool," declared Jocelyn, quite forgetting that she herself had come to London because she did not trust her sister's judgement.

"I have cast no aspersions on your sister's character," replied the Viscount. "She seems to me to be quite a gentle, amenable creature. I believe we shall deal quite well together."

"Oh, I'm sure you shall," returned Jocelyn, "especially if you browbeat her in your accustomed manner."

"My accustomed manner?" he repeated curtly.

"Yes! You come in and order her around as though she were a servant. It is quite abominable of you."

"I see." His lordship regarded her quizzically. "You believe that my treatment of your sister is not considerate."

"That," said Jocelyn, tossing her head angrily, her cheeks pink, "is an understatement. Quite probably in your own establishment you are used to ordering people about. But my sister, as you observed, is a gentle creature and is easily frightened."

"I assure you that I had no intention of frightening anyone – or being impolite," declared the Viscount, looking affronted.

"Then," said Jocelyn icily, "you quite

failed in your intention."

She found that she was glaring at him angrily and tried to calm herself.

The Viscount bowed his head, almost in acknowledgment of her rebuke. "I stand corrected," he said gravely, raising his dark eyes to meet hers. For several minutes he regarded her and Jocelyn felt herself coloring up. Finally he spoke. "You are quite a beautiful woman. I cannot conceive of your remaining unwed."

For a moment Jocelyn was left speechless. This was a subject she did not care to discuss. Then she answered sharply, "My marital status is no concern of yours. And I give you fair warning – I am here to see that Maria is allowed to choose her next husband – to please herself."

"She complained to you of me?"

"No." She thought the lie justified. She did not want him to scold Maria again.

"So what was *your* reason for coming?"

"To – to visit." Jocelyn saw the trap, but was unable to avoid it.

"I see. You came to visit – at precisely the time when your sister might expect suitors – merely as a coincidence." He raised a skeptical brow as he looked down at her through dark lashes.

Jocelyn felt herself coloring up again. "I

came to help my sister ... to protect her," she faltered.

The Viscount smiled, the first genuine smile Jocelyn had seen on his face. "To protect her from fortune hunters?"

She was forced to nod.

"Does not that indicate somewhat little faith in your sister's ability to judge character?"

"No," insisted Jocelyn, stubbornly conscious that her defense was weak. "Maria has a tendency to think well of people. That is all. She is perhaps too lenient with their failings."

"And you are not."

Jocelyn's respect for him was growing. The Viscount Ashburton was no easy opponent. Already she could see how he might use her admission against Maria when the truth of her sister's attachment to the tutor became evident.

"I am not lenient with men who seek to run women's lives for them. Maria married Mountcastle to please Papa. She was a good and faithful wife to him. I do not intend to see her forced into another such arrangement."

Ashburton frowned. "You are not much of a proponent for love."

There it was, thought Jocelyn, the implication that there must be something wrong with her because she was still unwed.

"I held out against my father," she declared. "I intended to marry someone I could love and respect. And I found no none who filled both these requirements."

The Viscount nodded. "It is obvious you have little use for men. No wonder you could find none to your liking. But tell me this – do you intend to speak against marriage to your sister?"

"Of course not." How little he listened, Jocelyn thought. "Maria needs a husband. I only intend to see that she gets one she wants."

"And I intend to see that she gets one who will care for her properly. Perhaps our aims are not so far apart. Perhaps we shall learn to deal together, after all."

"Perhaps," replied Jocelyn, but with the knowledge of Maria's attachment to Peter Ferris heavy in her heart, she was unable to put much enthusiasm into her voice. When his lordship discovered that Maria and Peter were devoted to each other, she hated to think what would happen.

"Jocelyn! Good morning. Good morning, milord." Maria's round face was more cheerful this morning, perhaps because she had just come from being with her Peter.

There was a sort of radiance about her. Jocelyn hoped the Viscount would not notice it.

"Good morning, milady. I hope I did not inconvenience you by arriving early last night."

Jocelyn just stopped herself from staring. The Viscount's tone was quietly courteous.

"Oh, no, milord," replied Maria. "It was quite all right. I hope everything was to your liking."

"Everything was satisfactory." His lordship's dark eyes sought Jocelyn's, almost as though he wished to see her reaction, then fell away. "Today I should like to speak to your steward, to take a look at the books, and examine the grounds."

"Of course, milord. I believe you will find everything in order. Mountcastle was quite pleased with Mr. Reever's work."

"I'm sure he was," replied the Viscount. "But this is a responsibility that he entrusted to me." His eyes sought Jocelyn's again momentarily. "You must understand that I wish to fulfill my uncle's wishes."

"Of course, milord. I do understand," answered Maria gently. "It is very kind of you to devote so much time to my affairs. I am sorry to be a burden to you."

"You are no burden," replied Ashburton

in so gentle a tone that Jocelyn almost gaped again.

"My uncle left you in my care – you and your sons – and I wish to do my best for you."

"Thank you, milord."

Jocelyn had noted the slight whitening of her sister's face. Maria, too, was not so naive as to expect Ashburton's approval of her wedding a tutor.

Just then the door opened and a footman entered, carrying a heavy tray. "Here is your breakfast, milord," said Maria. "Come," Maria touched her sister's arm. "Have your breakfast."

"And you, milady?" inquired the Viscount as he settled into a chair. "Have you eaten?"

"Oh, yes, milord." Jocelyn noted the slight flush that tinged her sister's cheeks and surmised that the tutor had also been present at Maria's breakfast.

As the footman seated her, she stifled a sigh. It must have been so pleasant for Maria and Peter and the boys, breakfasting together in contentment. Jocelyn could almost feel how pleasant, and she was condemned to eating with the Viscount.

Maria smiled at her again. "I have several tasks that need attending to. I shall see you later."

"Yes, Maria." Jocelyn, giving her attention

53

to the food before her, felt her spirits rising. A substantial meal might make the world seem brighter.

For some moments there was silence in the dining hall as the Viscount and Jocelyn both attended to their appetites.

The Viscount finished first and regarded her curiously, a brow lifted. "Did you find my recent behavior toward your sister more to your liking?"

Jocelyn nodded.

"But?" suggested his lordship, a hint of a smile on his lips.

"But I am not such a ninny as not to have discovered the persuasive effects of kindness. Probably as many women have been led into bad marriages by kindness as by anger."

"I see," said the Viscount consideringly. "You are not a particularly trusting person, Miss Franklin."

Jocelyn smiled coolly. "I am well aware of that, milord. Several years of caring for myself in a world run by men have disposed me to be somewhat suspicious."

The Viscount frowned. "How can you expect to find a husband if you regard all men as enemies?"

"I do not *expect* to find a husband," returned Jocelyn. "I am past the age of marrying. However, I do not regard all men as enemies – only those who think they know how to run my life."

"And would not a husband consider it part of his marital responsibility to help you make decisions regarding your life?"

"I suppose he would," replied Jocelyn thoughtfully. "And if I loved and respected him, and if he loved and respected me, then perhaps I should not find his help so odious."

"Perhaps," said his lordship. "But it has been my experience that women who run their own lives for long eventually become impossible to deal with."

"I think not," said Jocelyn rather sharply. "I collect that after all of these years of running your own affairs you would not take it kindly should someone suddenly arrive and begin telling you how to proceed."

"I certainly should not." Ashburton's eyebrows drew together at the thought.

"I suggest that a woman who has been running her own affairs for some time may have similar feelings. She is not impossible to deal with; she is merely accustomed to making her own decisions."

Ashburton considered this for some moments in silence. "Women are not competent to handle such things," he said finally. "They do not think in businesslike terms. They must be cared for and protected."

"You are merely repeating old lies," she replied. "If given the chance, a woman may handle her affairs every bit as competently as a man – perhaps more so."

Ashburton did not reply to this, but it was apparent that he did not agree.

"At any rate," said Jocelyn, "I do not intend to find a husband to manage my affairs."

"You may have suitors calling on you," he observed.

Jocelyn shrugged lightly. "That may be, but if I do, I shall know that it is probably my pocket that brought them."

The Viscount smiled at her. "For a woman who advocates love, you are surprisingly cynical."

"If I am, it is for good reason," replied Jocelyn. "I have had a great deal of experience with fortune hunters. Any suitors who come calling will soon discover that. I think most of them will not return again."

"Undoubtedly not," replied his lordship, "particularly if you deal with them as you have with me."

Jocelyn found herself smiling somewhat wickedly. "I was rather sharp with them," she reminisced. "But they deserved it. A man should be able to respond to a woman as to another human being endowed with some sense. This business of regarding women as helpless, brainless creatures is absurd."

A brief smile flitted over the Viscount's face, then was gone. "In one thing you are quite correct," he said.

Jocelyn stared at him. "And that is?"

"To regard *you* as helpless is truly absurd."

Jocelyn did not find this remark a felicitous one, but she forced herself to reply calmly. "Thank you, milord. I shall take that as a compliment."

"I thought you would," he replied quite seriously, then rose, and giving her a brief bow, strode from the room.

For a moment Jocelyn stood thinking. Then she made her way out the door and up the stairs. In this new mood the Viscount was even more irritating to her. She went to find Maria and warn her about men who were polite and friendly, especially men like the Viscount Ashburton.

Chapter 5

Jocelyn found Maria, as she had suspected, in the schoolroom with Peter and the boys. Her sister's face was aglow.

"I have come to ask if we might go shopping," said Jocelyn. "I am sadly in need of some new gowns – and bonnets."

Maria returned her sister's smile. "Of course, I shall take you to my dressmaker. In fact, I shall order the carriage for right after luncheon."

"Thank you," replied Jocelyn. "I believe I will feel somewhat more at home when I have more fashionable clothing."

"Of course you will," returned Maria.

"I think you are very pretty, Aunt," said Harold, looking up from his book. "You don't need any new gowns."

Jocelyn smiled. "Thank you, Harold. That was a lovely compliment."

Harold grinned. "That was not a compliment; that was the truth."

Jocelyn ruffled his hair. "Thank you, anyway, you scamp."

A small whining sound drew her attention once more to the boys. Spot's head was poking above the table. The boy had smuggled his pup into the schoolroom! Jocelyn wondered if the tutor was going to reprimand the boy for such behavior, but Mr. Ferris was merely smiling at the puppy's antics.

Jocelyn sent him a curious look. "Another of my idiosyncrasies," remarked the tutor mildly. "I see no harm in the boys having their pets with them. There is a great deal to be learned in caring for an animal."

Jocelyn shook her head. "Mr. Ferris, sometimes you are more than I can believe." She turned to her sister. "Maria, my dear, I cannot understand how you found such a gem."

Maria's radiant face reflected her pleasure in Jocelyn's compliments. "Mountcastle found him. He knew Peter's father."

"Did he also know Peter's philosophy?" asked Jocelyn, then regretted the question.

But Maria did not seem to mind it. "He knew a little, and Peter – Mr. Ferris – told him. Didn't you?"

Ferris nodded. "Lord Mountcastle had a great deal of concern for the education of his sons. We discussed it in great depth. His lordship seemed pleased with my plans for their education."

"Papa was very proud of us," said Tom solemnly. "He told us so right before – he went away." He dropped his eyes again to his book.

Maria's face softened. "I am quite sure your Papa was very proud of you both. But now you must get back to your lessons and Aunt Jocelyn and I must plan our shopping trip."

"Yes, Mama."

As Jocelyn followed her sister from the room, she could not avoid seeing the look that passed between her sister and the tutor. The boys were too young to understand the meaning of such a look, but Jocelyn was not. There was no mistaking the devotion that existed between Maria and Mr. Ferris.

The shopping consumed many hours. Jocelyn found herself ordering far more gowns than she had intended, but, she assured herself, they would last a long time, and she might as well enjoy herself while she was in London. If the Viscount's dark face flashed into her mind on more than one occasion, she dismissed it quickly; Ashburton had nothing at all to do with this.

She consulted the pattern books and with Maria's help decided on morning gowns of sprigged muslin, jaconet, and spotted cambric; a walking dress of sarcenet; evening gowns of silk, satin, and crape in shades of lavender, primrose yellow, and celestial blue. Then, just as they were about to leave, the dressmaker brought out a bolt of blue-green French silk of such sheerness that one could easily see the color of one's hand through the fabric.

"Oh!" cried Maria. "That is such a

beautiful shade. You must have a gown made of it."

It took very little persuasion before Jocelyn had ordered still another gown that she did not really need.

"Now to the milliner," said Jocelyn. "I must have something besides this dreadful bonnet."

At the milliner's she meant to be more circumspect, but somehow she ended up with more than she intended to buy. The new bonnets were much larger than her despised old Venetian one. She purchased a Gipsy hat of straw with a moderately wide brim which tied with wide white ribbons passing from the crown and curving the brim into a bonnet shape. There was something about its graceful shape and gentle curves that appealed to her. Then she debated over several capotes in silk and satin. They were quite similar, with their soft, puffed-out crowns and stiff brims framing her face. The white satin was adorned with rosettes of blue silk ribbon and tied with ribbons of matching color. She fancied it would go well with her new blue-sprigged muslin gown. But she also liked the other, which was slightly smaller and without ribbons. Its cream-colored crown sported a sculpted curl of bright feathers. Finally, she took them both, as well as a simple pale green toque for evening wear.

"I believe my present slippers will do, but I do need some new gloves," she told Maria as they returned to the carriage.

By the time they reached St. James's Square, the carriage was piled high with packages and Jocelyn was amazed at the extent of her purchases. "How could I have bought so much?" she exclaimed to Maria.

Her sister smiled at her. "Jocelyn, really, you did not buy a great deal. Ladies of the *ton* generally have many more gowns than you do. They think nothing of buying six or eight at a time, as well as bonnets, and gloves and slippers by the dozens."

"Yes, of course," replied Jocelyn. "But I am not a lady of the *ton*. I intend to go back to Sussex, you know. I do not need such fasionable gowns there."

Maria smiled. "Who knows, Jocelyn? Perhaps you will find a husband on this trip."

Jocelyn laughed. "I think not," she replied, pushing away that desire. "My days of thinking about a husband are over."

"Oh, Jocelyn, do not say that. Please!" Maria's voice betrayed her great emotion. "A woman needs lo—, that is, a husband."

For a moment Jocelyn thought her sister

was going to tell her about her partiality for Mr. Ferris, but Maria did not continue.

"Yes, Maria," said Jocelyn. "But you must realize, I am different from you. Men – I cannot find one that I can respect, let alone love."

"There are such men, Jocelyn, really there are. I mean – there must be."

Jocelyn nodded. "I'm certain that you will find someone whom you can love," she assured her sister. "I am here to see that the choice is *yours*."

"What if –" began Maria. "That is, Mountcastle was a Marquess. What if I should love someone who is not – not so high on the social scale?"

"If he were an honest man and loved and respected you, I do not think that should matter," replied Jocelyn, wishing that she could tell her sister that she knew the truth, but it was better to force Maria to tell her.

"What do you think Ashburton would say?"

"About a lord who was not a Marquess?" replied Jocelyn.

"Or – who was not a lord at all?" faltered Maria.

Jocelyn sighed. "I wish I could tell you that his lordship wishes for you to be happy above all else, but I cannot. The only thing I can

63

be sure of is that he will keep away fortune hunters."

"Oh, this man – I mean, I should not love a fortune hunter. I should know better than that."

Jocelyn patted her sister's arm. "Of course you should, Maria. Of course you should. When you find the man you love, please be assured that I shall be on your side, no matter what the man's class."

Maria smiled somewhat tremulously. "Oh, Jocelyn, you are such a comfort to me. I don't believe that I could stand up to the Viscount alone."

"Of course you could," replied Jocelyn firmly. "But it won't be necessary. For I am here, and I intend to stay until you are safely wed to the man of your choice."

"Oh, Jocelyn, thank you. Thank you so much."

"There is nothing to thank me for yet," replied Jocelyn. "Just be sure that you do not give in."

Maria's slender shoulders straightened. "Oh, I will not. I dare not ... not again."

By this time they had reached St. James's Square and there was no more time for talking. Loaded with boxes and bundles and followed by footmen with more, they made

64

their way up the path.

Rears held the door with his usual impassive look, yet Jocelyn sensed immediately that something was bothering him. In spite of his entirely dignified expression, there was about him an air of aggrieved martyrdom. She wondered momentarily if the Viscount had been harassing him. Then she followed Maria up the stairs.

They were met at the top by a scowling Ashburton. "Shopping, I see," he said in a voice heavy with displeasure.

"Yes," answered Jocelyn boldly. She was not afraid of the man, but to her anger he dismissed her comment and turned back to Maria.

"Is it not a little early," he inquired, "with the mourning only just down?"

Maria bowed her head. "I did not think of that, milord. I am sorry."

Jocelyn found herself bristling up. "Maria did not shop for herself. She went only to accompany me. Surely *I* may shop."

The Viscount regarded her sourly. "Of course you may shop. But a little forethought might have indicated to you that it would look ill for the Marchioness to be cavorting about Bond Street so soon."

Jocelyn felt her anger rising. How irritating this man could be! "We were not *cavorting!*"

she snapped. "We were shopping. Whatever blame there is is surely mine, not Maria's."

"You may take your share of the blame," returned Ashburton curtly. "But the Marchioness is not a child. She is as capable of correct thought as you."

"He is right, Jocelyn." Maria turned tear-filled eyes to her sister. "I have been lax in my respect to Mountcastle's memory. I am truly sorry."

"Your apology is accepted," said the Viscount with little grace. "When you have some time, I wish to speak to you about the maintenance of the house."

"Yes, yes, milord. After dinner?"

The Viscount nodded. "That should serve." He turned away brusquely.

"Milord!" cried Jocelyn, angered beyond reason by his top-lofty attitude. "*I* do not apologize."

"Jocelyn!"

"No, Maria. I refuse to apologize for a perfectly harmless shopping expedition."

The Viscount spun on his heel angrily and scowled at her. "I should not expect common decency from such as you," he returned. "You are concerned only with yourself."

"Oh!" Jocelyn found that she was trembling. The scene from her dream in which she had hurled the glass of wine at him

66

flashed before her eyes. How fortunate for the abominable Viscount that her sister was there, for if it had not been for Maria's restraining presence, thought Jocelyn, she might well have begun throwing her parcels at him.

As he strode angrily away, Jocelyn remained trembling with rage. She was so lost in it that Maria had to tug on her arm several times before she got her attention.

"Yes, yes, Maria. I am coming. But that man enrages me. How he enrages me!"

"There, there, Jocelyn. Do not let him bother you so. Come, we will put away your purchases. Perhaps his lordship has just had some bad news. By dinner he will be quite himself again."

"Himself!" snorted Jocelyn. "He *was* quite himself! An impossible, top-lofty, arrogant –"

"Hush, hush, Jocelyn. You must not speak so. Really, you must not."

Jocelyn let herself be led off to her room, but she was not at all mollified, and it was only to spare her sister's feelings that she did not for some time longer indulge herself in muttering recriminations against the Viscount.

Even when the parcels had been unwrapped and put away and Jocelyn had dressed for dinner, slipping on an old dress of pale blue

67

crape, as her new ones were not yet ready, she was still angry. How dare the man be so arrogant, so nasty? Who did he think he was, anyway? He might think that he could order Maria around, but not her. Nobody told *her* what to do.

It was this thought that was uppermost in her mind, giving color to her cheeks, as she made her way down the stairs sometime later. She was still angry, but she did not intend to let the Viscount know it. She would not give him that much satisfaction, she thought grimly.

At the bottom of the stairs she was met by a gently smiling Maria. "Oh, Jocelyn, how nice you look."

"I don't feel nice," she retorted.

"Please, Jocelyn, don't antagonize him any further."

"I have told you, Maria, the more you give in to men, the more they expect you to give in."

Maria's face saddened. "Jocelyn, please don't make him any angrier. I cannot stand it, truly I cannot."

Jocelyn was touched by her sister's obvious fear. "All right, Maria. I will contain myself, but only because of you. *He* deserves no consideration."

"For me, then – you will do it for me?"

"Yes, Maria, I will."

"Thank you."

"Where are you seating his lordship?" asked Jocelyn.

"He sits in Mountcastle's place," Maria said.

"And Mr. Ferris?"

"He – he will not be joining us tonight." Maria was obviously embarrassed by this. "He – he thought it would be best."

"But didn't he eat with you before?"

"Yes."

"Then mightn't Ashburton find this sus— strange?"

"I – I didn't think of that."

"Perhaps you should," returned Jocelyn.

"I – I think I will just go tell Mr. Ferris to come to the table, after all. I hadn't told Rears to change the settings yet."

"Kindly don't be long," said Jocelyn. "I don't wish to face his irascible lordship alone."

"Yes, yes," said Maria. "We'll be right back."

Maria sped up the stairs. She would be glad to have Mr. Ferris at the table, Jocelyn knew. She hoped that the two would know enough not to cast calves' eyes at each other. Ashburton would get on to them soon enough.

Jocelyn moved slowly toward the library.

Perhaps in there she would avoid Ashburton. She did not wish to face the Viscount alone. The man had such an unsettling effect on her. It was difficult to understand; she was unaccustomed to becoming so enraged.

Looking into the library, she saw that the room was deserted. She made her way to the bookshelves. Perhaps she could find something to read later to calm her troubled spirits. Her eyes moved over the titles. Mountcastle had been a well-read man, and kind. Maria had been fortunate in that. She had not been forced to live with a petty tyrant.

God help the woman who ever consented to be Ashburton's bride! No wonder the man had remained unmarried. No woman in her right mind would wish to be joined to such a moody, irascible man. His bad manners must have even turned away ambitious mamas, or perhaps the Viscount was a misogynist. It was certain that his estimation of womankind was not of the highest.

A pox on the Viscount! Jocelyn muttered silently. Could she never get that infernal man out of her thoughts? He intruded there with as little grace as he had intruded into the quiet, peaceful atmosphere of Maria's home.

Ashburton would always be regarded as an intruder, she thought. He would always disrupt the peace and comfort of those around him. Like many of the men she had known in the past years, he also seemed to be accustomed to getting his own way. She smiled grimly as she reached for a book. That was over now; the Viscount Ashburton was about to learn that the world was not run for his express benefit.

"Do you always smile with such maliciousness when you choose your reading material?" inquired a deep voice.

Jocelyn turned quickly. "No, milord. I was not aware that my smile *was* malicious."

His lordship leaned nonchalantly against the doorframe, gazing at her steadily through dark lashes. "Oh, it was quite malicious I assure you. I am an expert on malicious women, and I recognize their smiles quite easily." His own mouth curved slightly.

He was not angry; Jocelyn could see that. But she was not sure but that she would prefer his anger to this cool poise. For now his lordship was just watching her, there was nothing particularly offensive about it, yet she felt herself coloring up under the impact of those eyes. She was uncomfortably aware of the age of her dress. She could not, however, object to what was a standard way of behaving among the *ton*.

Jocelyn forced herself to smile. "Are you

always so complimentary to the ladies?" she inquired with a touch of sarcasm.

The Viscount laughed. "The ladies of the *ton* have no complaints about me."

"Then all I can say," returned Jocelyn sweetly, "is that the ladies of the *ton* are quite lacking in understanding."

Ashburton laughed. *"Touché,"* he said. "You have a sharp tongue."

"I do not deny that," replied Jocelyn. "It has served to quell meddling people who wished to interfere with my life." She raised a delicate brow pointedly.

The Viscount straightened. "Certainly I have no wish to do that."

Jocelyn tossed her head. "For someone who has no such wish, you have succeeded admirably well."

Ashburton's eyes gleamed. "I have? How?"

Suddenly Jocelyn saw where her anger had led her. "I . . . you have disrupted the peaceful atmosphere of this home," she faltered.

"And?" The Viscount prodded. "How have I interfered with *your* life?"

"You have not," she insisted.

"But you said that I had." The Viscount stepped closer until he was looking directly into her eyes.

Jocelyn felt the color rise to her cheeks

72

again. She certainly could not admit to this man how much he angered her, or how much of her time she spent thinking about him. He would surely misconstrue that.

"You mistake me, milord. I merely meant that your disrupting presence here also interferes with the quiet visit I had planned with my sister. And, of course, since I am close to my sister, what disturbs her also disturbs me."

The Viscount smiled. "I can hardly believe that a woman of your kind ever exists in quiet."

"Indeed, milord. I think that your acquaintance with women of my kind is rather limited."

Ashburton smiled. "Perhaps so. But in the weeks to come I shall certainly have the opportunity to learn, shall I not?"

Jocelyn looked down. She was not as calm as she hoped she appeared. His lordship was far too close to her for comfort. And, though he was taller than her by only several inches, he seemed to tower over her. Still, she refused to step backward. She would not let the man know that he could affect her so.

She drew herself as erect as possible, unknowingly presenting an enchanting picture – her hair escaping from its confines and her cheeks still pink from the force of her emotions. Her blue eyes were steady. "Milord, my only interest is helping my sister. To that end I am willing to work amicably with you. But if you attempt to browbeat her, to force her into anything against her will, I intend to fight you with every weapon I have."

For a long moment the Viscount held her gaze and then he smiled strangely, his eyes capturing hers. "Has anyone told you your curls are enchanting?" he asked in a low voice, reaching to tuck an unruly tendril back in place.

His touch was warm and Jocelyn found that her breath had suddenly deserted her. He was utterly impossible, this man. Could he never carry on a simple discussion? She was irritated with him, yet some deeply buried part of her admitted that she was pleased at his compliment.

For a moment, she searched her mind for some caustic reply, but none was forthcoming. Finally, afraid that he would see the response in her eyes, she spun on her heel and left him.

"It looks just as delightful from behind," he called after her, laughter in his voice.

But Jocelyn did not falter. Her back ramrod-straight, she made her exit. She dared not turn to look at him, for overriding her anger, and for no reason that she could fathom, she felt the strangest desire to laugh! Well, she would not do so. It was high time that Ashburton learned that all women were not silly, fragile creatures, easily bent to his will by the judicious use of a charming smile and a little flattery. She was made of sterner stuff; and that was most fortunate. For if she had not been, she might by now perhaps have fallen victim to the Viscount's quite viable charm, and that would never, never do.

Chapter 6

Jocelyn had recovered herself before they gathered for dinner, so she met the Viscount's level gaze with one of her own. Peter Ferris went to his accustomed place and the Viscount's dark face did not change expression. So, one hurdle was over. She breathed a sigh of relief. But it was only temporary. The Viscount, though he might be arrogant, was not stupid. Eventually, he would intercept a soft look between Peter and her sister, and then there would be an explosion. And what an explosion!

Jocelyn took her place at the great table. It put her directly across from the tutor. She saw that he was well, though conservatively, dressed. He smiled at her warmly as he took his seat. Jocelyn returned the smile. It took a man of courage even to contemplate what Peter Ferris was attempting, especially since he had already made his lordship's acquaintance. Any man who stood up to the Viscount was worthy of respect; that much was certain.

Jocelyn turned her attention to her sister. Maria's color was high and she looked uncomfortably flustered, but her hands did not tremble. There was very little conversation as the meal progressed. Maria was so thoroughly cowed that she barely raised her eyes from her plate. The Viscount, who seemed to be his morose and moody self, had little to say.

Jocelyn found the atmosphere quite oppressive. She could not help contrasting it to the pleasant meal of the evening before. There all had been accord and contentment; now all was gloom and discomfort.

Finally, she could stand the silence no longer and she spoke to Mr. Ferris. "I am looking forward to going to the theater. That is one of the few things which I miss while living in Sussex. Tell me, will Kemble be doing *Macbeth* early in the season? That is the one play I have promised myself I shall not miss."

"I believe that it is to be put on this fall, in the not too distant future, though I do not know the exact date. Of course, Mrs. Siddons will play Lady Macbeth."

"Have you seen it?" asked Jocelyn. She was well aware that his lordship was scowling, but she really did not care. If Mountcastle had thought Mr. Ferris fit to dine with, then Ashburton had no reason to complain. If a man was fit to sit at table, then it was certainly permissible to converse with him. In most circles good conversation at dinner was considered as important as good food. The Viscount, it appeared, did not believe so.

Both Jocelyn and the tutor left many opportunities for his lordship to join their conversation. However, he did not speak a single word, but attacked his food as though, Jocelyn thought, it had had the misfortune to offend him. Twenty-four hours in the same house with his lordship was enough to convince her that a more irritating, more surly man did not exist on the face of the earth. She was quite prepared to tell him so should the occasion arise.

During all of this, Maria was eating very little and looking at no one. Jocelyn found her anger rising. It was one thing for his lordship to tyrannize her and Mr. Ferris. They were made of sterner stuff and could withstand him, though not without some discomfort. Maria, however, was delicate and gentle and tender-hearted; she did not deserve his unpleasant behavior.

Finally, the dinner was over. The Viscount left his dessert, a tasty apple tart, more than half-uneaten. "I will see you in the library in ten minutes," he told a chastened Maria as he left the table.

There was silence as they listened to his steps go down the hall. Maria raised tear-filled eyes. "I expect he has found something wrong with the management of the house. Oh, dear, I thought everything was in order. I can't think what it could be."

"You have done everything to the best of your ability," soothed Mr. Ferris. "And you have done it quite well. His lordship can have no objections to that."

"Oh, he can. And he will – I know he will. I am so worried."

Jocelyn was feeling more and more outraged at Ashburton's brutal behavior. "Let me come with you, Maria."

Her sister shook her head. "No, Jocelyn, dear, that might anger him more. He does not

– That is, the two of you don't seem to deal well together."

"He does not like me," said Jocelyn. "That's what you were going to say, and it's quite true. I suppose he doesn't like anyone who refuses to see things his way."

"He is a lord," remarked Mr. Ferris calmly. "That is to be expected of him."

Jocelyn sighed. "It's too bad that your new beliefs have not spread further among the aristocracy."

"My beliefs are not new," said Mr. Ferris. "They are quite old. The aristocracy always used to be taught the right use of power, the idea that nobility obligates. *Noblesse oblige*, the Duc de Levis calls it in his *Maxims and Reflections*. But the idea itself is quite old, going back to Sophocles and Euripides."

Jocelyn was thoughtful. "How very interesting. Perhaps I should read that."

"I must go now," Maria said, her lip trembling. "Will you wait here for me?"

"Of course." Peter Ferris' devotion was clearly visible in the look he gave her sister, and Jocelyn felt a pang of envy. Oh, to be loved like that! She pushed the thought away – it was stupid to consider such a thing.

Jocelyn turned back to the table. "Well, Mr. Ferris, shall we discuss the education of young lords, or shall we pray for Maria's safe

79

return from the lion's den?"

Peter Ferris smiled faintly, preoccupied. "Milady is stronger than she looks. She will survive his lordship's tantrum, just as she did Mountcastle's. I only wish I might –" He stopped suddenly, aware that he had said too much.

Suddenly Jocelyn was tired of waiting. "Your secret is safe with me," she said. He looked at her with a start of surprise. "No, Maria did not tell me, but it is really not too difficult to see. When you look at each other with such tenderness, even Ashburton may begin to notice."

Peter Ferris frowned. "I feel so helpless. I love Maria, but I am not such a fool as to think that that will get me anywhere with the Viscount."

Jocelyn nodded. "I should think not. The Viscount, I suspect, has very little use for love."

"That is the least of our problems." Peter Ferris frowned. "If I had title or fortune, I could easily have Maria. But since I am a younger son, a tutor with little expectation, I am nothing in his eyes."

Jocelyn laid a comforting hand on his sleeve. "I don't want to give you false hope. I greatly fear that there will be a tremendous battle, but I assure you, Mr. Ferris, I am on your side. I came to London expressly to be by Maria at this time. My intent is to see that this time she marries to please herself."

Peter Ferris gaved her a warm smile. "You are an exceptional woman."

Jocelyn returned the smile. "In a certain sense I am free because Maria is not."

Mr. Ferris looked surprised. "I do not understand."

"I was thirteen when Maria married. Seeing her so frightened and pleading with Papa, I resolved that I would not marry unless I could find a man I could respect – and love."

"And you did not?"

Again Jocelyn felt that pang of loneliness. "I did not."

"You are still a young woman."

Jocelyn frowned. "My father gave me one season, and no more, to find a husband." She smiled. "Papa was a stubborn man, but he met his match in me."

Peter Ferris regarded her curiously. "You have never regretted it?"

"Well," replied Jocelyn, "while I do not exactly regret not having married, I do regret not having found someone I wished to marry."

He smiled sympathetically. "I believe I can understand that."

"I thought that you would." Peter Ferris

was really a good man, she thought. It was too bad she had not met a man like him before, during her season.

"I shall appreciate your help with his lordship," said the tutor, "but I must confess that I do not see a clear way. Every course of action that I contemplate seems equally unworkable." He shook his head. "If Maria were only a poor governess, I should devote my life to caring for her and the boys. But she is a Marchioness and well provided for. That makes it so much harder for me."

Jocelyn sighed. "I'm sure this will be no easy task. But I have learned –" Her lips curved slightly. "Through much experience with stubborn men, I have learned the value of patience. It has always been my practice to keep my composure. I eventually win, by simply persisting until I do."

Ferris smiled. "I imagine you have not run into many men like the Viscount."

Jocelyn nodded. "You are right about that. Most of my adversaries have been pompous old men. But I overcame them, and I will outlast the Viscount. Maria will not be forced to marry against her will; of that I am sure."

"Well," Peter Ferris did not seem particularly reassured, but Jocelyn could not blame him. Anyone with a modicum of sense who stood up against the Viscount would realize that he faced a formidable opponent. "Well," he repeated, "I can only do my best."

"Don't despair, Mr. Ferris." Jocelyn felt a real need to see the man smile. "We will figure out some way. We simply must."

Peter Ferris nodded.

The sound of heels in the hall made them both look up. It was the tutor who sprang to his feet first and reached Maria's side. Then he seemed to realize his predicament and did not reach out to touch her.

Maria's fair face was flushed and tear-stained and she was twisting her handkerchief between nervous fingers. "He thinks the servants are lax. And he says – he says the boys are not being properly educated. And – there was more, but I cannot remember. And Jocelyn, he wants to see you."

"Indeed!" Jocelyn found her bristles up already. The Viscount would not reduce *her* to tears.

"Mr. Ferris, I suggest you take Maria up to her room, where she may lie down for a while. I am going to see his lordship." She exchanged a significant glance with the tutor and saw that he, too, was anxious that Maria be comforted.

She straightened her back determinedly. Ashburton could browbeat Maria, but he would not browbeat her.

As she made her way toward the library, she took several deep breaths. Above all she must keep her composure. She would not let Ashburton anger her again. Nor would she respond to him if he fell into the laconic pose of the beau. She could not be moved by the false compliments of exquisites and dandies. She wondered what it was his lordship wished to discuss with her. Perhaps he intended to take her to task again for the shopping trip. How foolish the man was and how concerned about the opinion of the *ton*. That boded ill for the future, she thought sadly.

She entered the library with her head high. The Viscount had his back to the door. She was struck by the strength of the shoulders revealed in his well cut coat, and she scolded herself. This was hardly the time to observe that his lordship was an attractive man. He might have broad shoulders, but he certainly had a narrow mind!

"You wished to speak to me?" Jocelyn said sweetly, looking at him demurely from under her lashes.

Ashburton spun around to face her. "Yes, I do."

Jocelyn smiled. "I am here, ready to listen."

"I do not find this situation amusing," he said sharply.

Jocelyn spread her hands. "Since I do not know what situation we are discussing, I am unable to say."

The Viscount frowned.

Jocelyn maintained a bland and amiable expression. "Since I have no idea how long this discussion will take, I believe I will make myself comfortable, if you don't mind."

Ashburton said nothing, but his scowl did not diminish.

Jocelyn moved easily into the room and settled herself in a chair. She took her time getting comfortable in it. Then she turned to the Viscount. "Now, milord, what is it you have to say to me?"

"I think you should go back to Sussex."

Jocelyn bit back a gasp of surprise. He certainly did not waste any words.

"Really?" she replied, striving still for a sweet tone, though she could feel her anger building. "And what has brought you to this startling conclusion?"

"Your sister does not need your company. I am quite capable of seeing her well settled."

"Indeed." Jocelyn had some trouble remembering her resolution to remain calm. Never had she known such an irritating man. "Indeed, milord, that may be your opinion. However," she pointed out, "I believe that we have somewhat different ideas on what constitutes 'well settled.' "

"I do not wish to bandy words with you," replied the Viscount autocratically. "I find your presence here disrupting to the entire household."

"*My* presence!" exclaimed Jocelyn, thinking of the peaceful atmosphere that had prevailed in the house before his lordship's arrival.

"Yes, your presence. You brought two puppies into the house, upsetting the boys' education. You should have known better than that."

"The puppies are not upsetting anything." Jocelyn refrained from repeating Mr. Ferris' remarks on the value of caring for animals. It was best to leave him out of this.

"You are upsetting your sister – undoubtedly putting ideas of rebellion in her head."

"I am not!" declared Jocelyn. "I have only encouraged her to uphold her rights."

"I believe that I am better prepared to judge what is good for her than you are," he replied.

"I do not think so!" cried Jocelyn indignantly. "I have promised myself that my sister will please herself in her choice of a husband this time. And I intend to stay here and see that she does."

"You are a bad example to her," said his lordship curtly.

"Because I counsel her to stand up for what she wants?" Jocelyn was getting angrier and angrier. How dare he say such things? As though he were God Himself!

"You are a poor example of womankind for several reasons," replied Ashburton. "You might also consider the indiscretion of carrying on with the tutor. Undoubtedly, the man is aware of the extent of your fortune, but it ill befits a woman like you to marry such a man."

This time Jocelyn sprang to her feet. There was no way to conceal the anger that was coursing through her. She approached until she was quite close to the Viscount and then she stared into his dark eyes. "You, sir," she said icily, "are offensive. Because I treat a man with common courtesy, a man your uncle thought fit to educate his sons and have dine at his table, is no reason to insult me. I assure you that Mr. Ferris has no interest in me in the way you seem to think, nor I in him. In the future I shall thank you to keep your ill-bred tongue out of my affairs. I shall speak to *whomever* I please, *whenever* I please. Praise God, I must not answer to such as you for my actions."

By the time she had finished this speech,

she was angrier than she had ever been in her life. Under her thin gown her breasts rose and fell with the force of her rage. She found that her hands were clenched into tight fists. Ashburton returned her glare without flinching. For a long moment he held her gaze and then encompassed her slender form with a look. He smiled, a harsh smile that seemed to chill her blood. "I suggest that you look higher than Peter Ferris for a husband," he said slowly. "You do have a certain amount of – money."

This was too much for Jocelyn. Something snapped inside her, and quite without her willing it, her open palm flew up and connected with his cheek. His lordship did not move. His eyes held hers, their expression unreadable while the white mark of her hand appeared on his dark skin.

Jocelyn stood for a moment, aghast at the lengths to which her anger had driven her, and yet perversely pleased that she had struck him. Then she started to turn away.

"Not yet," declared Ashburton, grasping her arm, his autocratic face set in harsh lines.

Jocelyn knew she could not escape his grip and she forced herself to face him without flinching.

"It is seldom that a woman has struck me in anger." His tone was silky as he looked down at her. "And never *before* I had kissed her." His eyes moved slowly over her face and he seemed to be debating something within himself.

Jocelyn attempted to free herself, her heart pounding, her dark curls tumbling in disarray and her cheeks growing rosy with the effort. But it was all useless; his grip was like iron.

"You are a bully," she began as he drew her closer, "an arrogant, tyran –"

His lips cut off her words and she ceased struggling, forcing herself to stand in the cold apathy that had so effectively discouraged her unwanted suitors. But this was a kiss like none she had ever known. It shook her very depths and she did not know how much longer she could remain icy when suddenly he put her from him.

"You are capable of anger, but your heart is frozen," he mocked. "You have forgotten the graces of womanhood."

Jocelyn forced her numbed brain to work. "And you, sir, have certainly forgotten the manners of a gentleman. Release me instantly."

"Of course." He dropped his hands awkwardly.

Jocelyn stopped herself from swinging at him again. She must get away from this man who so infuriated her so she could think clearly.

"Of one thing you can be certain," she said grimly. "No matter how you insult me, I intend to stay here and stand by my sister. Nothing you do or say will change my mind about that."

Ashburton made no reply to this. His dark features were set and withdrawn, but his eyes seemed almost puzzled as he regarded her.

Jocelyn stared into them for a long moment, then swung angrily on her heel and hurried from the room. How dare he kiss her like that! It was as though he thought he could overpower her as a woman. Then, when she did not respond to that type of coercion, to dare to suggest that she was frozen! Never in her life had she so desired to commit violence against another human being.

Chapter 7

In the next two days Jocelyn's irritation with Ashburton did not abate. He did nothing to increase it, except that he gave her no occasion to voice it. When he met her in the halls of the great house, he invariably nodded politely and passed on, though sometimes she surprised an intent look. Surely there was no reason to take umbrage at this, yet she did. She did not quite know how to deal with this politeness of his. It made her ill at ease. It also angered her excessively to find that she colored up under his look; no matter what she did or told herself, she could not stop her cheeks from flooding scarlet when his eyes lit on her.

Finally, she had decided that her only defense was indifference. The decision, however, was not a particularly great help to her, since she was unable to act upon it. The mere sight of Ashburton's lean form seemed to annoy her.

"You must not let him upset you so," said Maria to her sister as they returned from a drive in Hyde Park. "He means well. Surely you know that. It is just his way."

"His way!" cried Jocelyn. "Oh! He makes me so angry I feel like kicking him! Maria, the man is impossible!"

"I'm sorry, Jocelyn, really I am. But you know there's nothing I can do. Mountcastle made him my legal guardian. He controls my money. There is no way at all that I can ask him to leave."

Jocelyn sighed. "I know that, my dear, but he irritates me so."

91

Maria smiled gently. "He is not a very tactful man, I know. But he really does mean well."

Jocelyn stared at her sister. "Mean well?"

"Of course. He does want to fill the trust that Mountcastle left him. The poor man cannot help it if he has such a rough nature. I know for a fact that he has spent hours going over the books here. His own establishment in Dover is run extremely well and with a great deal of concern for the welfare of the servants. He recently pensioned off his butler and suggested that I give some thought to the future pensioning of Rears. He is a good man, Jocelyn, even though he frightens me."

Jocelyn shook her head. "What a sweet creature you are, Maria! You are always looking for the good in people."

Maria smiled again. "There is good in everyone, Jocelyn. You know that."

Jocelyn shook her head again. "Perhaps, but I have yet to find any in his lordship." Still she smiled. She knew that Maria would keep insisting on his lordship's goodness, and so she changed the subject. "The pups seem to be adjusting well, don't you think?"

"Yes. Mr. Ferris says so. And the boys are so pleased."

Jocelyn nodded. "Your Mr. Ferris is a fine man. You are fortunate in your choice."

Maria dimpled prettily. Though her sister had known the secret for several days, Maria still had a tendency to flush when they talked about the tutor. "Yes, he is. Oh, Jocelyn, I do not see how I can have been so fortunate. He is such a wonderful person."

Jocelyn did not like to dampen her sister's high spirits, but she knew they must face reality. "You will hold out against Ashburton, won't you?"

Maria's gentle features hardened. "I will marry no one but Peter Ferris. No one – ever."

"Good," declared Jocelyn. "I am counting on you not to lose your nerve."

"I shan't, Jocelyn. Oh, I shan't!"

Maria's face changed suddenly. It paled and then it was flushed with sudden color. "Good day, milord," she faltered.

Jocelyn swung around. Ashburton was standing in the doorway. His tall, lean body seemed to emanate arrogance. His eyes slipped over her and then returned to her sister.

"I have been addressed by several prospective suitors," he said evenly. "The first will come calling today. He is Baron Hegers."

"B-but, milord," faltered Maria, "so soon? The mourning is just over. I – I do not wish to receive suitors just yet."

The Viscount's handsome features took on a granite look. "The mourning is over. You must get on with living. Hegers is a sound man – substantial – with few bad habits." He glared at Jocelyn. "He does not gamble and he is past the age of – other pursuits."

"How – how old is he?" Maria's face had paled again.

"He is somewhat younger than Mountcastle was."

The Viscount seemed purposely evasive. Jocelyn bit her tongue to keep from asking the natural next question – how much younger? Let Maria ask him.

But Maria did not ask; Maria stood, trembling like a leaf in a November wind. "I will receive him," she replied.

"Good. I trust you will consider the future of your sons. Hegers is a good man. He would treat you well."

Maria nodded. She seemed unable to speak further.

The Viscount turned to Jocelyn. "I trust that you will not permit your aversion for men to interfere with the settling of your sister's future."

His tone was even enough, but it held a certain menace and Jocelyn dug her nails deep into her palms to control her anger.

"I do not hold *all* men in aversion," she replied coldly, "only those who attempt to interfere with other people's lives." Her look was pointed and she heard Maria gasp, but anger overrode caution. "I have told you more than once, had you cared to pay attention to me, that my concern for Maria's future does not include turning her against men. I wish to see her safely married to a man of *her* choice."

Ashburton smiled coldly, not giving an inch. "Perhaps she will choose Hegers."

"Perhaps," replied Jocelyn, striving to keep her tone from betraying her knowledge of Maria's love. This was not the time to even think about the fact that Maria had already made her choice – and that that choice was a tutor!

"Has Miss Franklin told you that I suggested that she return to Sussex?" the Viscount asked Maria.

Maria's pale cheeks colored again. "No, milord, but perhaps she knew that I should take exception to your saying such a thing."

Jocelyn stared at her sister in amazement. She had never seen Maria in so determined a mood before.

Ashburton scowled. "Already she has changed you."

Maria shook her head. "No, milord, she has not. I have never approved of an invited guest receiving insult in my house."

Jocelyn was surprised to see Ashburton wince. Did the mighty Viscount have feelings, then? And could those feelings really be touched?

"If I have insulted your sister, I beg your pardon." Ashburton spoke hesitantly and addressed Maria. "I am attempting to fulfill the charge that my uncle left me. I have never before had to supervise women. I find the task difficult."

Jocelyn was about to reply with a sharp remark, but a glance at Maria's distressed face stopped her. She forced herself to speak calmly. "I accept your apology, milord."

Maria gave her a grateful look and Jocelyn kept her face steady, not allowing the triumph she felt to show in her features. Ashburton had actually apologized!

The Viscount seemed somewhat disconcerted by his actions. "I have business with my steward and Mountcastle's," he said to Maria. "I trust you can deal with Hegers' visit without me."

"Yes, milord. Will you be here for dinner?"

"No. Tonight I dine out. My maiden aunts have insisted on my presence. I am not in London often; my affairs in Dover usually take up most of my time. Now that I am in the city, they are capitalizing upon it." He straightened his shoulders as though facing something unpleasant, and added almost as if explaining to himself, "They raised me, and so I owe them a debt of gratitude. Doubly so, because they do not go into society."

In spite of his words, something in his voice alerted Jocelyn to the fact that Ashburton did not look forward to this visit. Her mind began to speculate on the life of a small boy raised by two austere maiden ladies.

He spoke again in his usual arrogant voice. "In the morning I shall speak to you about Hegers."

"Yes, milord," replied Maria.

Ashburton turned, his eyes avoiding Jocelyn. She watched him stride away, swinging along with a grace that characterized his every movement. There was no denying that Ashburton was a well-favored man. But that, of course, did nothing to lessen his conceit.

"Jocelyn." She grew aware that Maria was tugging at her arm.

"Yes, Maria, I hear you." Jocelyn forced her attention back to her sister.

"Oh, Jocelyn, it's beginning." Maria clutched at her. "What shall I do?"

Jocelyn patted her sister's hand. "You will do just as we planned. You will meet your suitors civilly and kindly, then reject them."

97

Maria nodded. "Yes. I know. But that seems so – so dishonest. If only we could come right out with it and tell the Viscount the truth."

Jocelyn shook her head. "That's exactly what we must not do. You must wear down the Viscount. You must be patient. You must meet each suitor and find something wrong with him – something legitimate."

"I know," Maria nodded. "But I long so to be Mr. Ferris' wife. I don't want to wait."

Jocelyn nodded. "I know, my dear. But you must be patient."

Maria managed a smile. "Peter says that, too. But it is so difficult."

"Yes, but it must be done. Come, let us take a breath of air in the courtyard before your caller comes."

Maria nodded. "Yes, let's; that will calm me. You will stay with me, won't you? You won't leave me alone with this man?"

Jocelyn smiled. "Of course not. I will be there every moment. Have no fear about that."

They met Peter Ferris as they walked in the courtyard among the summer flowers. "Oh, Mr. Ferris!" Maria cried.

He reached out a steadying hand to touch her. "What is it, milady?"

"It's – it's –" Maria seemed suddenly

unable to continue.

"She's trying to tell you that her first suitor is coming calling today."

"I see." Peter Ferris spoke calmly but his agitation was evident in his face. "Well, you must do as we planned."

"Yes, yes, I know. But I do so long –"

Jocelyn laid a detaining hand on her sister's arm. "Maria, my dear, you will get your wish. I promise you. But we must follow our plan."

"Yes, Jocelyn, I know. I will do as we agreed."

"Good." Jocelyn smiled. "Now you must get along without me for a while. I have some letters to write. But I shall be with you long before the Baron arrives. Rest assured of that."

As she made her way into the house and up the stairs, she was aware of a great sense of emptiness inside her. Why was it that the sight of Maria with her beloved Peter gave her such a terrible feeling of emptiness? She had long ago decided that the love she had once believed in finding was never going to be a reality; there was no sense now in wasting time with vain regrets.

Besides, if she had married any of her suitors – the boring Sir Firley or the odious Mr. Ancton, for instance – they would both be extremely sorry by now. There was no sense in allowing herself to feel sad. She would feel joy in Maria's happiness and forget her own unfulfilled dreams. Let the irritating Ashburton keep his insults to himself, she thought, suddenly angry. She could have had a husband had she wanted one.

When she came down the stairs some time later, she carried her needlepoint with her. She had begun a set of chair covers for the dining room at home in Sussex, and she had brought them along to London with her. She would have something to keep her hands occupied while Maria made conversation with Lord Hegers. Something about doing needlework was comforting to her; it had a calming effect on her nerves, which were overwrought lately because of the disquieting presence of his lordship in the house.

A sound man, Ashburton had said of the Baron. Jocelyn almost snorted aloud. She wished now that she had asked his lordship directly what the Baron's age was. He had been far too evasive about the whole thing. She would not like this Baron; Jocelyn felt fairly sure of that. If Ashburton approved of him, then there must be something wrong with him. She was aware that her reasoning in this matter was somewhat faulty, but she did not care.

Maria was already in the drawing room. She turned from her nervous pacing back and forth to look at her sister. "Oh, Jocelyn, there you are. I'm so terribly nervous. You'd think I was about to come out."

Jocelyn chuckled. "Come, Maria. You are a grown woman, a mother. There's no need for you to be so jumpy."

"I know, I know. But I still am."

Jocelyn put a restraining hand on her sister's arm. "Maria, my dear, do sit down." She drew her sister toward the divan. "Come and look at my needlepoint. Tell me what you think of the design."

Jocelyn succeeded by this ruse in diverting her sister's attention to the needlepoint, and so when Rears announced the Baron, Maria was able to look up with something like calm. "Show him in, Rears."

"Yes, milady." Jocelyn could not help watching the door as avidly as her sister. She was extremely curious as to what sort of man the Viscount found suitable for Maria.

She bit her bottom lip as the visitor entered. He was certainly not a beau. He was short and round. Even the Regent's staymaker could not have succeeded in containing the belly that strained against his brightly striped waistcoat. His head was almost as round as his belly and the bald top of it shone brightly between two fringes of sparse brown hair.

"Marchioness," said the little man.

"Lord Hegers." Maria was on her feet, quite calm and collected, Jocelyn noted. "Won't you sit down?"

'Thank you, milady."

The little man seemed ill at ease. Perspiration stood out on his forehead and gleamed on his bald spot. He licked his lips nervously.

"Perhaps you would care for a glass of wine or a cup of tea?" offered Maria, obviously so concerned for the little man's comfort that she had quite forgotten her own fears.

"Yes, yes, tea if you please, milady," the Baron mumbled as he settled himself in a graceful lyre-back chair. Jocelyn gave her attention to her needlepoint. In the dainty chair the little man looked even more ridiculous. Jocelyn, in an effort to keep down her laughter, stabbed her finger and winced.

The Baron regarded her with concern.

"This is my sister, Miss Jocelyn Franklin. She has come to pay me a visit."

"Of course, of course." The Baron essayed a bow. Sitting as he was, it was not at all succesful. Jocelyn stabbed herself again in an effort not to laugh. She hoped Maria's suitors would not all be so hard on her fingers.

Maria went to the bell pull. "Some tea,

Rears," she told the butler when he appeared. Then she settled again beside her sister on the divan.

Jocelyn, devoting herself to the needlepoint, listened while her sister strove to make conversation with the Baron. But her every opening remark was answered by a few mumbled phrases – the same phrases, as far as Jocelyn could tell.

Fortunately, the tea arrived, and Jocelyn, eyeing the Baron over the rim of her Wedgwood cup, saw that he, too, was relieved by having something to do with his hands. She passed him the macaroons.

"Thank you, Miss Franklin."

Jocelyn, watching as crumbs collected on the waistcoat, began to like the little man. He was not, of course, a suitable husband for Maria, whether or not she had formed a previous partiality for Peter Ferris. But he was so obviously uncomfortable in the role of suitor that she could not help commiserating with him.

Maria evidently felt the same way, for she endeavored to draw the little man out. "I hear that you have recently purchased a new house."

The Baron nodded. "Yes. On Grosvenor Square." He shifted a little uncomfortably in his chair. "I hope to take my bride there."

Maria colored slightly and Jocelyn rushed into the gap with the first thing she could think of. "Is it a new house? That is, just built? Or is it one of Robert Adam's?"

The Baron's face lit up as though he had just spotted a dear friend. "It is an Adam house," he said enthusiastically. "It is partly for that reason that I purchased it. But the main reason was the wrought-iron work." A beatific smile wreathed his round features. "It is superb. Absolutely superb."

"Do you fancy wrought-iron work?" asked Jocelyn.

"Ah, yes!" The Baron gave a great sigh of pleasure. "Have you an interest in the art?" he asked, eagerly turning to face her.

"Indeed, I have." Jocelyn leaned forward in her chair. "My father used to take me along when he went to inspect some of the best work. Have you seen that on Lord Corning's house? Papa used to admire it excessively – the balconies in particular."

The Baron smiled. "No, I have not. I shall go tomorrow to see it. Thank you for that information, Miss Franklin." Now that there was a topic of conversation he not only was interested in, but knew something about, the Baron opened up like a blossoming flower. He was filled with enthusiasm and they discussed architecture and wrought iron at length.

Some time later when the Baron consulted his time-piece, Jocelyn was as amazed as he to find how the time had sped. "I shall call again – soon, I hope," he said, giving a warm smile to Jocelyn. Then he rose and, paying his respects to Maria, made his way from the room.

As the door closed behind him, Maria began to giggle. "Oh, Jocelyn, you've no idea how serious you looked, as if the art of making wrought iron was of the utmost importance."

Jocelyn smiled. "Well," she said defensively, "iron *is* very interesting. And it certainly did pass the time."

She sobered as she and Maria returned to their places on the divan. Actually, the Baron would make a good husband for a certain sort of woman. Had she been forced into a loveless marriage, she might well have chosen a man like him. Even Maria, had she not loved Mr. Ferris, might have found life with the Baron pleasant.

"Oh, Jocelyn, it seems so unkind to let him come again when we know –"

Jocelyn silenced her sister. "We must give ourselves time. We need to find something wrong with the Baron, something that Ashburton will recognize. Obviously, he has already seen the man and does not regard his appearance as important."

Maria nodded. "I believe the Viscount is being very selective about those he allows to call. Peter heard from Rears that he refused several fortune hunters permission to call. He is trying to protect me, and the Baron seems a nice, pleasant man. You liked him."

"I did," agreed Jocelyn. "But I should not like to have him for a husband."

"No, nor I," Maria hastened to agree. "I was merely commenting on his lordship's actions."

Jocelyn nodded sagely. "I still think you are far too good-natured for your own benefit. You are always thinking of others."

Maria colored. "I only wanted you to see that his lordship is not such a terribly bad person."

"That," said Jocelyn as she gathered her needlepoint and prepared to return to her room, "is something I reserve judgment on. When I see you safely married, then I shall concede that he is not all bad."

Chapter 8

The next morning did not find Jocelyn feeling any differently about the Viscount. In fact, the pleasant dinner hour that she had spent the night before with Maria and Peter Ferris had only renewed her wish that his lordship would leave them to live in peace. That, of course, was not to be, at least not without a great deal of effort on their part.

Jocelyn was clad in one of her new gowns, a creation of yellow sprigged muslin with full sleeves and skirt trimmed with *rouleaux* of muslin and dark yellow ribbon that made her feel much younger than her spinsterish two and twenty. Her hair was confined simply, in plaits, with light ringlets about her face. She waited in the breakfast room for Maria to return. Maria had promised to hold firm to her resolution, but Jocelyn was still somewhat concerned. Maria had such a pliant disposition.

As she sipped at her chocolate and nibbled absent-mindedly at a muffin, she hoped that Ashburton wouldn't be too hard on Maria. Could the man really have supposed that her sister would be content with the Baron?

Jocelyn recalled Maria's words of the day before. It was not surprising to her that several undesirable men had approached the Viscount. Maria's substance was considerable, and it was understandable that a man of the world should consider the support of two children a small price to pay for control of it. What was rather surprising was the Viscount's reported vehemence in turning away such men. He obviously made a distinction between these men and the Baron. Though Hegers was also interested in Maria's money, an alliance with him would give her a secure and respected future. It would be an even exchange. Perhaps she had misjudged him in this one thing, thought Jocelyn. Maybe he really did find the task of caring for Maria a difficult one.

Still, she felt her anger rising again; that did not excuse his irritating actions toward herself. She was most incensed by the memory of that degrading kiss. The man was so arrogant that he thought a kiss could win over any woman. Then because she refused to melt in his arms as he had evidently expected, he had accused her of being frozen. Frozen! Jocelyn could feel her anger against the man building and building.

She finished the muffin and picked delicately at the crumbs on the cloth. It

108

was still a mystery to her why his lordship's presence should make her so angry, but there was no denying that it did. If only Maria and Peter Ferris were safely married and she could return to the old house in Sussex. It was ordinary there, sometimes even dull, but there was no disquieting Ashburton to agitate her. Perhaps once she got away from the sight of Maria's and Peter's devotion to each other, she would be able to banish the feelings of envy and sadness that she sometimes felt. Jocelyn sighed. She had never been a moody person. Seldom had she known long periods of sadness or anger. She had always faced life with a certain sense of competence. There might well be difficulties in her life; there often had been. But from that day as a thirteen-year-old when she had decided to be the mistress of her own affairs, she had let no obstacle deter her. She had not always succeeded in getting what she wanted, but she had never allowed anyone to force her to do anything against her will. She had always faced the world with cheerful confidence, certain that she would remain her own mistress.

Now she seemed to have lost control. She was either seething with anger over Ashburton's outrageous behavior or filled with vague, indefinable longing. She did not like this state of affairs and was not used to having her emotions out of control. The whole situation made her extremely uncomfortable.

She debated about having another cup of chocolate but decided against it. Certainly Maria would not be immured with Ashburton much longer. A sound in the doorway made her look up. A tremulous Maria stood there. She was not weeping, but she was perilously close to it. Jocelyn rose hastily and hurried to her sister's side. "Maria, what is it?"

"Come up to my room, Jocelyn. He may come in here."

"Yes, of course. Right away."

Jocelyn said no more as they hurried up the stairs and into the safety of Maria's room. She settled her sister on a divan and sat beside her. "Now, Maria, tell me what that horrible man said. Did he insist that you accept Hegers?"

Maria shook her head. "No, no, he was quite nice about that. He seemed annoyed about something, but it wasn't that."

"Then what is it?" Jocelyn eyed her sister with concern.

"He said – He said –" Maria stopped, obviously overcome with emotion. "He said I must hire a new tutor. He does not approve of – Mr. Ferris!"

"My God!" The exclamation escaped Jocelyn before she could stop it. "What did you tell him?"

110

"I – I told him that Mountcastle had hired Mr. Ferris, that he had discussed his teaching with him, and that he approved of it."

"And?"

"He did not believe me. He said that it wasn't fitting for Mr. Ferris to dine with us, to – to be with us at table. He seemed angered by our simple conversations."

Jocelyn frowned. "That doesn't seem sufficient reason to dismiss a tutor."

"That's what I told him, but he didn't seem to care. He just kept saying that I must dismiss him."

"And you said?" Jocelyn prompted.

"I said I could not do such a thing. I could not go against Mountcastle's last wishes."

"Very good."

"But it didn't help. He said he would no longer pay Mr. Ferris' wages. Oh, Jocelyn, we did not think about this happening."

"No, we did not. But we will handle it. You haven't seen Mr. Ferris yet, have you?"

"No. I came straight to you."

"Good. Don't tell him he's dismissed."

"But, Jocelyn, it's almost quarter day. If the Viscount does not give me the money, I cannot pay Mr. Ferris."

"I will give you the money."

"But, Jocelyn, I cannot take your funds."

"You can – and you will," Jocelyn said

firmly. "Money is only worth having if it helps you achieve your ends. You may repay me later if you wish."

"But, Jocelyn –"

"If you tell Mr. Ferris the truth, will he not feel compelled to leave?"

Numbly, Maria nodded.

"Then do it my way; it will give us a little longer."

"Yes, Jocelyn. But, oh, I don't know how we shall manage. If he disapproves of Mr. Ferris as a tutor, how can he approve of him as a husband?"

"We must simply wear him down," Jocelyn declared. "You keep refusing every offer. He has said that he finds this task uncomfortable. Eventually, he will tire of it and let you do the choosing."

Maria sighed forlornly. "I hope you are right, Jocelyn. I really do."

"Of course I am right." She said this with more confidence than she felt. Her own run-ins with the Viscount had not always been successful, but she did not know any other way to proceed.

There came a gentle tap at the door. Maria dabbed hastily at her eyes. "Yes?"

The maid, Rose, opened the door. "It's his lordship, milady. He wants to see you, Miss."

"Thank you, Rose. I'll be there shortly."

As the door shut, Jocelyn turned to her sister. "You lie on your bed for a while and compose yourself. You cannot let Mr. Ferris see you like this. And I will go see his lordship."

Maria grabbed her sister's arm. "Please, Jocelyn, do not make matters worse."

Jocelyn shook her head. "I don't see how things can be much worse, but I promise to control myself. Don't worry." She detached herself from Maria's grasp. "Do not concern yourself, please. Just lie down and rest a while."

As she made her way down the stairs, she could already feel herself tightening up. The anger that she felt toward his lordship seemed always to be seething inside her, ready to boil over at a moment's notice. Well, this time she would not allow it. She would remain quite calm no matter what impossible thing he chose to say to her. She would simply refuse to allow him to ignite her anger. By this time she had reached the library and to her annoyance she found that her knees were trembling. This was insupportable. She was certainly not afraid of the Viscount Ashburton – or twenty like him.

She straightened her shoulders and stepped into the room. "You wish to see me?"

The Viscount turned from a painting he

was regarding. "Yes, I do."

Jocelyn advanced into the room and gave him what she hoped was a calm glance. "I fail to see what you may have to say to me," she began.

Ashburton's face darkened. "You often fail to regard what I have to say to you."

"That," replied Jocelyn stiffly, "is because you insist on interfering where you have no right."

Ashburton's scowl deepened. "I have every right. My uncle left me a sacred trust. I am merely attempting to fulfill it."

"Your uncle," returned Jocelyn icily, "left you no trust in regard to me. I am perfectly capable of running my own life."

"I do not wish to interfere with your life," retorted his lordship, "though it appears to me that you have made rather a mess of it."

Jocelyn found that her hands had curled into fists and she was breathing heavily.

"You should have married," he continued. "Then perhaps you might have known happiness."

Jocelyn bristled. "My happiness is no concern of yours!" she cried. "And I would have been miserable married."

"Not to the right man," declared the Viscount stubbornly.

"And what," asked Jocelyn derisively, "constitutes the right man?"

Ashburton smiled, a surprisingly wicked smile. "What you need is a strong man, one who could master you."

"Master me!" Jocelyn found to her distress that she had stamped her foot like a child.

"Yes, it would take a strong man, but it could be done. Only then would you be happy."

Jocelyn stamped her foot again. "You are impossible, sir. I assure you, no man will ever master me."

The Viscount watched her, his gaze lingering on the fashionably low-cut bodice of her muslin gown. She felt the telltale scarlet rush to her cheeks. For a long moment he stared at her while she fought vainly to control her rage. "Contrary to your present belief, I did not request your presence in order to incur your anger," he said finally.

"Then why –" asked Jocelyn.

"I have just informed the Marchioness that the tutor must be dismissed and a new one be hired."

"That was ill considered of you." Jocelyn was still battling her anger. "Mr. Ferris is doing an excellent job with the boys. Your uncle approved of him."

Ashburton frowned. "I am aware that my

uncle hired the man, but I think that he made a mistake."

"A mistake?"

"The man is a fortune hunter."

"A fortune hunter? Peter Ferris?" Jocelyn's tone revealed her amazement.

The Viscount smiled sardonically. "You have not been very observant. Mr. Ferris has been extremely gracious to you."

"To me?" Jocelyn sank into a chair, her mind a mass of confusion.

His lordship shrugged and said cuttingly, "You have been so taken up by Mr. Ferris' charming attentions to you that you have missed his intent."

Jocelyn felt the hysterical laughter rising in her throat. How blind could his lordship be? "I – I assure you, milord, that Mr. Ferris has no intent in regard to me, no intent at all. Nor have I at any time considered Mr. Ferris in the light of a prospective husband. I thought I had settled that before."

It was obvious to her that his lordship did not believe her. The scowl on his face did not lighten and he continued as though he had not heard her. "I have informed the Marchioness that Mr. Ferris is to be dismissed. I will help her engage another tutor."

"You are being unfair!" she cried, springing to her feet. "Grossly unfair! And

116

– And –" She stopped suddenly. She could not tell the Viscount that she intended to pay Peter Ferris' wages; that would only confirm him in his suspicions.

"Yes?" asked Ashburton, a curiously bleak look in his eye.

"I do not think Maria will dismiss the tutor."

"I think the man will not stay long when he discovers that no wages are forthcoming."

"You are an abominable man!" cried Jocelyn. "I do not know how anyone can stand you."

The Viscount frowned. "My reputation among the *ton* has never been in dispute."

Jocelyn smiled acidly. "My opinion has not previously been consulted."

Ashburton's scowl grew darker and he snapped, "I do not know how my disposition got dragged into this. But no matter. I have made up my mind about Ferris. I suggest that you look elsewhere for a husband."

"I *told* you –" began Jocelyn.

"And I told *you*," replied the Viscount. "I will not countenance this man pursuing your fortune while I am around to stop it."

"Oh! How can you be such a fool?" cried Jocelyn. "I do not need the likes of you to protect me. Why don't you leave this house,

117

where you have ruined what was once an atmosphere of pleasant calm? Why don't you go back to the ladies of the *ton* and let them extoll your virtues? They seem to be able to appreciate you."

"I do not need your advice about how to run my life," said the Viscount stonily. "You are meddling."

"I?" Jocelyn's anger seemed to be throbbing through her whole person. "Perhaps now you see how I feel at your interference. Why can you take it upon yourself to run my life, but I cannot direct yours?"

"You are a woman," replied Ashburton curtly.

"And so, supposed to be without proper understanding."

The Viscount smiled unpleasantly. "That is the general conception."

"It is wrong!" cried Jocelyn. "It is grossly unfair. A woman's brain is no different from a man's."

"Indeed!" returned the Viscount. "The law does not seem to believe so. The law considers a woman to be a child in need of guidance."

"The law is wrong!" cried Jocelyn. "There are many women with just as much understanding as men. There would be more if they were allowed the same sort of education."

His lordship snorted in disgust. "What a lot of nonsense. Men have always run the world."

"And rather poorly," snapped Jocelyn.

Ashburton grimaced. "There is little use in wasting your breath in trying to convince me of such addle-brained things."

"There is little use in talking to you about anything," declared Jocelyn hotly. "You are so puffed up with a sense of your own importance that you think of no one but yourself. And you admit nothing that does not fit with your limited views of the world."

Ashburton glared at her. "If you find my company so reprehensible, why don't you return to Sussex? We should both benefit by it."

"I will not leave Maria in your clutches, to be disposed of like a piece of merchandise. I warn you, Ashburton, do not interfere in my life, and do not attempt to coerce my sister. I will not stand for it."

She turned on her heel and moved toward the door, but suddenly he was in front of her. "Just a moment, Miss Franklin."

She attempted to move around him, but his hand closed on her wrist. "You have vented your spleen on me; now I will have my say. I have a trust from my uncle. I intend to fulfill it to the best of my ability. I am a man, with a man's sense of responsibility. I do not intend to let fortune hunters marry your sister, or you, for that matter, while you are in this house. You may grow as angry as you like, but I intend to do things as I see fit."

Jocelyn's wrist throbbed from the pressure of his grip, but she continued to face him.

"We are at war, milord; that is evident. You are physically stronger than I." She glanced at his hand on her wrist. "You may detain me by physical force, but you will never make me change my mind."

Ashburton laughed harshly. "I was right. What you need is a man with a strong hand – a good spanking is what you need."

Jocelyn gasped. "You have no right!"

"Oh, no?" Then the Viscount smiled mischievously. "I do not intend to undertake the task of taming such a shrew."

Jocelyn felt herself trembling with rage. It was only with the greatest effort that she kept herself from swinging at him with her free hand. For a long moment their eyes held. Then the Viscount released her wrist and turned his back on her.

Dismissed! she thought angrily. Dismissed like a scolded child. For a moment she considered addressing him again, but she realized that it would do no good. So, gathering her dignity as best she could, she made her way from the room. Almost blindly she climbed the stairs and closed herself into her chamber. There she threw herself on the curtained bed and tried to dissipate the anger that consumed her.

Never, never in her life had she met such a man. He drove her to distraction with his arrogant, top-lofty ways. Why now, of all times, must she long for that most impossible of all things – to be loved?

Chapter 9

A state of armed truce seemed to exist between Jocelyn and the Viscount for the next several days. By mutual agreement the two of them avoided each other's company. Jocelyn took to peeking into the hall to see if the coast was clear before she ventured out of her room. The first time she discovered herself doing this, she stamped off down the hall in a veritable dudgeon. Then she realized that it was only sensible to avoid such a man.

She and Maria kept busy. They went shopping, returned the calls of several ladies, and visited Somerset House.

By diligent effort she managed to avoid being alone with the Viscount. And then Maria announced that he was going to his house in Dover and would be out of the city for several days.

Jocelyn breathed a great sigh of relief. "What a blessing!" she exclaimed. "Perhaps we can have a little peace and quiet now."

"Hush, Jocelyn, please." Maria's hands trembled as she tried to quiet her sister. "I do not want him to hear you."

The last days had taken their toll of Maria. It was quite clear to Jocelyn that her sister was distraught by Ashburton's refusal to pay the tutor's wages and fearful that Peter Ferris would discover the true state of affairs. So far this had not happened, but Jocelyn could see that her sister lived in constant fear of it. Maria's face seemed to grow paler every day and her hands trembled constantly.

"He says that a new suitor will be coming – the Marquess of Marston."

"A man of equal rank," mused Jocelyn.

"Yes. And I'm frightened. Oh, Jocelyn, I wish we might have told Ashburton the truth. It seems to me that would have been more honest."

"Perhaps, Maria. I cannot say." Jocelyn was not used to admitting defeat, but she had never before met a man like the Viscount. All her hard-won knowledge of how to get her way seemed useless where he was concerned. "We will have a few days of rest while he's gone. We can think and plan then, and you, my dear, must stop letting the Viscount upset you so. You are not looking well."

"I'm doing the best I can, Jocelyn. I am not strong like you. I try my best, truly I do, but it is so hard. The Viscount, when he glares at me, reminds me so of Papa. I feel just like a tiny little girl, hardly able to answer."

"But you are not a little girl," said Jocelyn in soothing tones. "And once we convince the Viscount that you won't give in, then you will have things the way you please. You and Mr. Ferris will be happily married."

Maria sighed. "Oh, Jocelyn, I don't know anymore. Sometimes that seems like a dream, a beautiful dream that will never come true. Sometimes I feel that I am just fooling myself, that I will never be Mr. Ferris' wife. The Viscount – perhaps he is too strong for me."

"Maria! You must not say such things." Jocelyn was surprised at the strength of the dismay she felt. "You do love Mr. Ferris?"

"Of course I do," Maria replied.

"Then you must not think of giving him up. If I had someone to love, who loved me, why – why I should die before I gave him up."

In utter amazement Jocelyn stood while the tears rolled down her cheeks. Why had her voice broken like that? And why had she said such an outlandish thing? To die for a man's love! Why, it was outrageous even to feel such a thing! And even more outrageous to have *said* it! Jocelyn Franklin voicing such a sentiment!

"I – I'm sorry, Maria," she said. "That was a ridiculous thing for me to say. Anyway, there's no need to talk of dying, or of giving up."

"Oh, Jocelyn, I didn't know. I'm so sorry."

"Sorry? About what?"

"That you have loved someone and lost him."

"But I haven't!" cried Jocelyn. "Really, Maria, I have never loved a man. I – I do not know what has come over me."

It was Maria's turn to speak soothing words. "It's all right, Jocelyn. These past days have been hard on you, your fighting with Ashburton and all. I'm sorry to be such a burden to you."

"Nonsense." Jocelyn wiped furiously at the tears. "You are not a burden. This is your life we are talking about."

"Now, Jocelyn, please, I will feel better about this, really I will. Don't worry about me."

"All right, Maria. Listen, I have some things to do in my room. But I'll come down before the Marquess arrives. Do you know him?"

Maria shook her head. "No. Mountcastle and I did not go into society often. He liked a more peaceful life."

Jocelyn nodded. "Well, then we shall just have to wait to see what Marston looks like ... until later." She squeezed her sister's hand and made her way up the stairs to her room.

Tears! It was incomprehensible that she should be reduced to tears – and over what? She wasn't quite sure. Certainly she believed a woman should hold out for the man she wanted, but it was quite another thing to be reduced to sentimental tears and talk of dying!

The constant presence of that irritating Ashburton had unstrung her nerves more than she realized. What a blessing it would be to have him gone and be able to breathe freely and walk about the house without the fear of having those sardonic black eyes fasten upon her.

She reached her room and crossed it to stare into the cheval glass. A tear-stained face did nothing to improve her looks. It was fortunate that she had reached her room without encountering his lordship. One more arrogant look from him and she would simply scream.

She stared at herself in horror. Where was the calm, confident young woman who had entered this house just a few short weeks before, who had never let a man interfere in her life? She turned away from the glass with a sigh and made her way to the divan. Absently she picked up her needlepoint. The chair covers were not progressing well. She always seemed too busy or too nervous to work on them. The usual comforting effect of stitching was no longer there. She could only stitch for a moment or two; then inevitably she would either prick her finger or cast the work aside to pace nervously up and down.

Perhaps Maria was right. They may have made a mistake in not declaring their position immediately. Yet, what good would that have done? The Viscount was hard 'as rock. It was inconceivable that he should have been pleased at Maria's preference for the tutor. No, she was sure they had taken what seemed the best course.

She gave an exclamation of pain as the needle stuck her finger and threw the offending cover aside. On the other hand, she thought as she sucked her finger, it might be time to reconsider. After Maria met and rejected this Marston and Ashburton returned from his trip, perhaps that would be the time to speak. They would have to wait and see.

Some time later Jocelyn descended to the drawing room. The needlework had been left behind. She was far too nervous to want to work on it. This fact was even more unsettling than the nervousness itself. Never in her adult life – which had begun when she was thirteen – had she found herself unable to do something that she knew would be of benefit to herself. It was quite unsettling, she reflected as she moved into the drawing room, to have so lost control of one's self. She did not like it at all.

"Ah, Jocelyn, there you are."

Maria looked quite lovely in a dress of green-spotted cambric, her fair hair pulled back simply. Her face was a little pale, but she seemed more relaxed than she had for some time. Her hands did not tremble at all as she arranged some pale pink roses in a vase.

"I'm glad to see that you are looking better," Jocelyn commented.

Maria flushed a little but continued her task. "I am much calmer now. His lordship has gone and will not return till Friday."

"Four whole days!" cried Jocelyn in relief. "Oh, it will be heavenly!"

Maria frowned. "I hope it is not wicked of us to be so jubilant."

"Nonsense, my dear. We have the right to rejoice at our good fortune. After all, it is not as though we wished his lordship any harm."

Maria's face brightened. "That is right. And it would be hypocritical of us to pretend what we do not feel."

"You are quite correct, Maria. We have every right to enjoy his absence."

It looked as though Maria might contest this, but before she could answer there came a deferential tap on the door.

"Yes?"

"The Marquess of Marston has arrived," intoned Rears.

Jocelyn stifled a smile. The butler's dignity was at times a trifle excessive. When the caller appeared in the doorway, however, she was pleased that her expression was suitably sober, for the Marquess was dressed completely in black; even his cravat was black. Jocelyn looked him over carefully. He was a tall man, and thin, but not with the lean, lithe grace of a man like Ashburton. He moved stiffly, as though not certain that the body he commanded would really obey him.

"Marquess," said Maria graciously, but with trembling lips.

Jocelyn sighed. Maria was already terrified of the man.

"Milady." Stiffly, the Marquess kissed Maria's fingers. Then he straightened and regarded Jocelyn with critical eyes.

"This is my sister, milord – Miss Jocelyn Franklin."

The Marquess gave Jocelyn a cursory look and then turned back to Maria. So, thought Jocelyn, the Marquess could not be bothered with her. Well, that was good. Her first evaluation of him had not been especially favorable, either.

"Your sister is somewhat beyond the marriageable age," he remarked.

Jocelyn felt herself bristling immediately. Another man who thought he knew everything!

"I suppose, though, that we can find her a husband."

"That will hardly be necessary, milord," Jocelyn said evenly.

"It will be no trouble. I have many friends." The solemn Marquess said this with obvious satisfaction.

With difficulty Jocelyn kept her temper in hand. "I meant, milord, that I do not wish to have a husband."

The Marquess frowned. "Nonsense, my dear. Every woman wishes to have a husband.

Is that not true, milady?" He turned to Maria.

"I – I cannot say, milord," Maria faltered. "Perhaps most women do. But not –"

"Nonsense. Once your sister has a husband, she will leave all these ridiculous ideas behind her. I shall make her betrothal my first task."

At this the Marquess sat down and looked very pleased with himself.

Jocelyn hardly knew whether to laugh or cry. How could the man be so deaf? Could he not conceive of a woman who did not want to be leg-shackled to a man?

"I think you mistake yourself, milord," she said in as even a tone as she could muster. "I do not have a husband because I do not *wish* to have a husband. Any effort by you in that regard would be a complete and utter waste of time."

For a moment the Marquess seemed taken aback. And then he smiled, the smug smile of a man who thinks he holds the upper hand. "We shall speak to your guardian about the matter. I'm sure he will be sensible."

It was with the greatest pleasure conceivable that Jocelyn looked the Marquess straight in the eye and replied sweetly, "I have no guardian, milord."

"No guardian! Such a thing is impossible!"

The Marquess looked as though someone had informed him that horses had wings.

Jocelyn shook her head. "Your knowledge of the law is faulty, milord. I have no male relatives and my father left my fortune in my own keeping."

"Lunacy!" declared the Marquess. "Sheer lunacy!"

"I assure you that the whole thing is entirely legal and proper. I am my own mistress, and I intend to stay that way."

The Marquess looked extremely uncomfortable for several moments, but then seemed to dismiss the matter. He turned to Maria. "I understand you have two sons?"

"Yes, milord. Fine boys."

"I see, I see. Well, undoubtedly they are young rascals and need a strong hand to keep them in line. But never fear, I am equal to the task."

Maria regarded the Marquess with cold eyes. "My sons are very well-behaved young gentlemen. They do not need to be kept in line."

"Yes, of course, of course. Merely an expression," the Marquess said nervously.

There was a long period of uncomfortable silence. Maria, Jocelyn saw, was not going to do anything to help the Marquess, and neither was she. Finally, he consulted his timepiece. "My, my, how time flies. Must be going."

"Good day, milord," replied Maria with such coolness that Jocelyn almost smiled. Where her sons were concerned, Maria would brook no interference. Every word that the Marquess had spoken had made him a more unlikely candidate.

Coolly, the two women watched Marston leave and then they turned to each other in relief.

"What an insulting man," observed Maria.

Jocelyn laughed. "I noted that you did not defend me from him. It was only concern for your sons that aroused you."

Maria chuckled. "There was no need to protect you, Jocelyn. In fact, it might have been kinder to protect the Marquess. You did rather unsettle him."

Jocelyn snorted. "I should hope so! The man needed to be jarred out of that asinine smugness." She smiled in satisfaction and tilted her head. "And I think we succeeded in that."

"Oh, yes," agreed Maria. "He was most definitely unsettled. But, Jocelyn, do you suppose that he will tell Ashburton how we treated him?"

"What if he does? The Viscount expects such behavior from me. He would be surprised if I treated your suitors with excessive courtesy, and you certainly have the right to defend your sons. They *are* well behaved."

Maria smiled weakly. "I do not like to have my boys maligned, especially now that –" She stopped and flushed.

Jocelyn laughed. "Come, Maria, you may as well finish your sentence, especially now that they are Peter's charge."

Maria flushed even more. "But he has done wonders with them, Jocelyn. Even Mountcastle said so. And Mr. Ferris was only here a few weeks before –"

"I know, Maria. Please, do not distress yourself over Lord Marston. If he is not put off by today, you will just continue to refuse him."

"Yes, I suppose so. I only hope that the Viscount is not too upset by it."

Jocelyn shrugged. "Forget his lordship. Let us have a few days of peace and contentment. I am really exhausted by these constant altercations with Ashburton."

"He seems to have formed a particular dislike for you," mused Maria.

Jocelyn laughed. "I suppose that he has. He came here expecting to find a sacrificial lamb, a willing one. Now he has found the lamb unwilling, with a lion in attendance, as well."

Maria laughed. "Jocelyn, I wonder

sometimes how we can be sisters. How very different we are. Why, anyone would think that you were the elder. Here I am six and twenty and still feeling like a schoolroom miss, and at two and twenty you are running your own life." Maria's face saddened. "Tell me truthfully, Jocelyn, do you never yearn for a man to do things for you?"

Jocelyn laughed and shook her head. "Indeed, I do not! I know very well what I'm about and how to take care of myself."

"But –" Maria hesitated as though unsure whether to continue. "But don't you get lonely without someone to love?"

For a moment Jocelyn was tempted to lie, but then she sighed. "Yes, Maria, I do. But even if I had such a man, I should hesitate to put my affairs in his hands."

"You should? Whatever for? If you loved him –"

Jocelyn felt that she would be unsuccessful, but she attempted to explain her feelings to her sister. "I have run my affairs for so long that I should feel diminished by giving them up to another's control; I would feel less of a person."

It was obvious from Maria's bewildered frown that she did not understand this sort of thinking. Jocelyn smiled. "Don't worry about it, dear. It is just one of my eccentricities."

Maria did not smile. "I do not worry about you handling your own affairs, for I know you are quite capable of that. But I do worry that you have no one to love. What I feel for Mr. Ferris is so wonderful!" Maria's face took on that radiance that seemed to emanate from it whenever she spoke of her Peter.

"I should like to love someone, Maria," replied Jocelyn seriously. "But I have found no one I could love. I cannot love just anyone."

Maria considered this for a moment. "I know, Jocelyn. It's just that I'm so happy. I want you to have happiness like that."

Jocelyn forced herself to sound cheerful. "Don't worry, Maria. We will settle your affairs first. Who knows? Perhaps the right man for me will turn up." She put as much enthusiasm as possible into her voice. There was little point in depressing Maria by telling her what Jocelyn was certain of – that she doubted there would ever be a man whom she could love. She had acknowledged this fact to herself, but she still did not feel peacefully resigned.

She was still musing on this when the children burst into the room, chattering excitedly. Jocelyn suppressed a smile. It was fortunate that the Marquess was not present to witness this confirmation of his ideas.

"Tom, Harold, whatever are you talking about?" demanded Maria over the babble.

"Guess what, Mama, guess what?"

Maria smiled. "I'm sure I can't guess, Harold. Tell me, what is it?"

"We are going to Astley's, to the Amphitheatre, tomorrow afternoon. Oh, Mama, it will be such fun."

Tom, mindful of his position as Marquess, spoke with more dignity. "Mr. Ferris says there is a great deal to be learned there. They put on mock battles, you know, and the horses are wonderfully trained."

Jocelyn sighed. "Yes, I've heard so. How I should love to go. I have never been there. Papa would not allow it."

"Perhaps," said Mr. Ferris from the doorway, "perhaps you and milady would care to accompany us?"

For a moment Jocelyn hesitated, but just for a moment. Then, giving young Harold a wink, she declared, "Oh, I should love to go. What a capital idea!"

Maria, only too glad to go anywhere with her beloved Mr. Ferris, nodded her confirmation.

Chapter 10

The whole of the next day seemed given over to preparations for the Amphitheatre. By the time they were ready to leave, Jocelyn found herself as excited as the boys. She had chosen a dress of blue sprigged muslin and wore the white bonnet trimmed with blue rosettes. She felt like a schoolgirl on a holiday, she realized as they gathered in the hallway to wait for the carriage. It was an exhilarating feeling to be doing something besides avoiding the Viscount. It was too bad, she said to herself, that the overbearing snob couldn't just stay away permanently. Life was so pleasant in his absence.

While Harold and Tom plied Mr. Ferris with questions about Astley's, Jocelyn watched her sister. Maria's color was high and a radiance shone in her face. How dense the Viscount was not to have detected the devotion that existed between Maria and the tutor.

Finally, Rears announced, "The carriage is here, milady."

With a great deal of confusion and repeated requests from the boys to have someone look

137

in on the pups lest they get lonely, the little group made its way to the carriage. Jocelyn, catching a tender look between Maria and Mr. Ferris as the latter helped her sister to her seat, felt a sense of loss. How stupid, she told herself, and utterly vexing, too, to be feeling loss for someone she had never had. She would stop it immediately.

She smiled brightly at the others. This was a day to enjoy. The Viscount was far away and they were free to have a little fun, and she fully intended to do just that. "Have you been to Astley's before?" she asked her sister.

Maria shook her head. "No. Mountcastle was always very busy. He preferred that we stay at home."

Jocelyn nodded. Mountcastle had cared for his wife, but he had never thought to arrange his life to gratify any of her wishes. He most probably had not even considered that she might have any.

Jocelyn stifled a sigh. This was no time to get upset over the condition of woman, nor was it sensible to make generalizations about the male half of the species. Still, a great many of them were completely ignorant of the women in their care. They, like the condescending Ashburton, were convinced that they knew best how to run a woman's life. Well, she would show his high and

138

mighty lordship precisely how mistaken he was. She would –

She brought herself up sharply. She meant to enjoy this period of peace. Why must that insolent man keep invading her thoughts? She wished that she never need consider him again, but it seemed that whenever her mind was not actively engaged in some definite task, he immediately forced his way back into it.

They had taken the open carriage and Tom and Harold kept calling out in excitement at the various sights they saw. Mr. Ferris seemed to be enjoying their excitement as much as they were, pointing out other things for them to notice.

Jocelyn turned to look at her sister. Maria's gentle face was lit with a beatific smile as she regarded the man she had given her heart to and the children they both loved. "You are absolutely radiant today, Maria. You look ravishing."

Maria flushed. "Hush, Jocelyn. I know I am not striking like you. If I look well, it must be due to the fresh air."

Jocelyn smiled, but made no further reply. She knew Maria did not want the boys to be aware yet of her partiality for Mr. Ferris. Anyone who spent any time in their presence must be aware of it. No matter how studiously they avoided each other's eyes, there was something in the very air when they were together. Certainly on some level the boys were aware of something, and their affection for their tutor was evident.

Yes, thought Jocelyn, anyone could sense the depths of their affection, anyone except the puffed-up Viscount. Then she grimaced in distaste. There he was again, interjecting his unwanted presence into her thoughts!

By this time they were approaching Westminster Bridge and the Amphitheatre. It was apparent from the throngs that many people intended to enjoy the circus that day. Maria looked out into the teeming mass and paled.

"Do not be alarmed, milady," said Peter Ferris. "They are all friendly people. I shall hold tightly to one hand of each of the boys, and each of you will hold the other. I have taken a nice box for us."

Tom and Harold needed no second invitation to clamber down, but they waited patiently by the carriage until their mother and aunt had been helped to descend. Then, following the tutor, they made their way into the building.

In a surprisingly short time they were seated in the box and the boys were hanging over the front, exclaiming over everything

140

that came into view. Jocelyn caught Mr. Ferris' eye and he smiled. "The task of becoming a gentleman is an arduous one," he declared. "And we have only one childhood. Children learn better if they are permitted some play."

Jocelyn returned his smile. "You are a very wise man, Mr. Ferris."

The tutor's smile faded. "In matters of education, perhaps, but in other matters –" He shook his head.

Jocelyn did not need further words to know that he was thinking of the inadvisability of a tutor wishing to become the husband of a Marchioness. She summoned her brightest smile. "Never fear. We shall prevail."

"I hope there will be a battle," said Harold. "Do you think there will be, sir?"

Peter Ferris smiled. "The advertisement promised quite a grand mock battle with charging horses."

"Oh, that will be capital, sir!" cried Harold.

"Look, Harold!" cried Tom. "The orchestra is beginning to play." Above the babble of the happy crowd rose the rousing sound of martial music. Jocelyn felt a stirring in her blood; how invigorating the music was. She looked around with interest. The Amphitheatre was decorated with fanciful designs, and an immense glass chandelier

141

suspended from the middle of the building cast its light over the whole spectacle.

"I understand that Mr. Astley, Jr., is responsible for the decoration," observed Mr. Ferris. "A man of some talent. He also is responsible for painting the stage scenery."

"The circus has been here a long time, has it not?" inquired Maria.

"This structure," explained the tutor, "is the third and most sumptuous. It is relatively new, built in 1804. The other two were destroyed by fire."

"I wonder what made the elder Mr. Astley think of such an enterprise."

"I have done some reading with the end in mind of being able to answer any questions the boys might raise," replied the tutor. "Mr. Astley, Sr., learned horsemanship in the army. He was a well-known equestrian. He seemed to have had a great love for horses and greatly respected their intelligence. Just wait until you see his horses do a country dance. You would swear they were enjoying it just as people might."

Jocelyn smiled. She had always been fond of animals and she looked forward to watching the horses perform.

"At one time Astley had his circus in Paris, but the Revolution caused him to come back to England," said Peter Ferris.

"Oh, look!" cried Harold. "Look!"

Jocelyn brought her attention back to the equestrian ring. The ringmaster had just entered, resplendent in his coat and flowing white stock, his long whip trailing behind him in the sawdust. The boys stared in awe as several mounted horses thundered into the ring.

"Oh!" The boys seemed frozen as they watched. At a signal from the ringmaster, the horses began to trot around the circle in tandem. Then slowly and gracefully each rider got to his feet on the horse's back. They kept their places with as much ease as though they stood on solid earth as the horses, at the ringmaster's command, changed pace. Then, while the boys watched in agony and Maria gasped aloud, the riders changed horses! As calmly as if they were crossing the street, they switched their positions. With wide grins they bowed gracefully to each other and then to the wildly clapping audience, while all the time the horses continued to circle the ring.

Jocelyn smiled at the boys' amazement. They watched each move with mouths wide open. Even Jocelyn herself couldn't help holding her breath as the riders stood, each on one foot, moving with the animals' gait and then slipped down to upend themselves and continue the ride on their heads!

"Oh, Mr. Ferris!" cried Tom, never for a moment removing his eyes from the wonderful sight before him. "I shall never forget this. Not as long as I live."

"Me, either," breathed Harold. Maria and Mr. Ferris exchanged a laughing and tender glance.

The horses and riders left the ring and half a dozen terriers decked in great colorful bows on their collars and matching gauze skirts around their middles followed a pretty young girl into the ring. She, too, wore pink gauze, tights, and spangles. The dogs arranged themselves in a neat circle around the girl and waited. She whistled softly and at her signal the dogs all rose on their hind legs and began to pirouette around her. Harold turned to Tom. "I wonder if we can teach Spot and Samson to do that," he said to his brother.

"I don't know." Tom was grinning. "But it would be fun to try."

Jocelyn stifled a chuckle. Tomorrow the pups would have a busy day, and since bulldogs were built somewhat differently from terriers, the boys might find their task rather difficult.

Jocelyn watched with interest as the trained dogs did their tricks. The crowd roared its approval as the terriers danced in pairs,

144

jumped through a hoop, and lay down and played dead. They were quite well trained, thought Jocelyn, wondering vaguely what sort of life the young girl led.

What had impelled her to become part of a circus? It must be a very different life from Jocelyn's. Idly, she wondered if men tried to manage that girl's life. Were the men in the circus as overbearing and arrogant as Ashburton? That hardly seemed possible.

The dogs followed their mistress out of the ring and were succeeded by a troop of gaily dressed tumblers. As they tumbled over each other and performed various tricks, Jocelyn smiled to herself. Undoubtedly tomorrow the schoolroom would see the boys attempting something similar. Since there were only the two of them, however, they would fortunately be unable to duplicate the human pyramid four men high with which the tumblers ended their act. The tumblers were followed by two brightly painted clowns who threw buckets of water on each other, and threatened the audience – with buckets that turned out to hold only sawdust.

During the final altercation between the clowns, a dappled white horse entered the ring. Perched on its back was a small monkey. The little creature sat on a brightly decorated saddle and seemed to enjoy the applause that greeted its arrival. It wore a brightly spangled red jacket, blue trousers, and a red cap. Standing up on the saddle, it bowed to the audience, right and left, and then as the ringmaster directed, the horse with its monkey rider circled the ring. The monkey seemed to enjoy the adulation of the crowd as it leaped with agility through a hoop and regained its balance on the horse's neck.

Harold turned to his mother. "Mama, that's what I want for my birthday. I want that monkey."

Maria turned startled eyes to the tutor. Mr. Ferris smiled at the boys. "That would be rather hard on Spot and Samson, don't you think? They may not understand if you bring home another pet."

"I didn't think about that."

"Also," added Jocelyn, "the monkey might not like to leave his friends. He seems very happy here."

Tom nodded. "I don't think he would like to leave the circus. It must be lots of fun to be here every day."

Jocelyn and the tutor nodded.

How good Mr. Ferris was for the children, thought Jocelyn. He knew how to reach the boys. He was an admirable man, not like that – She stopped herself sharply. She

146

would not think about Ashburton. She simply would not.

The boys were clapping excitedly as Jocelyn returned her attention to the ring. She would be hard put to tell which act the boys liked best, but when the arena was cleared for the big spectacle, and horses, carrying armed riders, came galloping into the circle, she knew that it would be this that would engage the boys' attention for weeks afterward. The martial music, the beating drums, the pounding hooves, the clashing swords – all these reverberated through the air and the boys bounced excitedly on their seats in front of her. "Look, oh, look! Look at that one!"

"Oh, it fell!" cried Tom, with a frightened look at the tutor.

"It's all right, Tom. The horses are trained to fall. They don't get hurt."

"Not at all?" asked Harold.

"Not at all," assured Peter Ferris. "They practice a great deal, horses and riders both. No one gets hurt."

"It looks so real," breathed Maria.

"Of course," replied the tutor. "They work very hard to make it look that way. Many of these riders have been trained as equestrians since their early youth."

"That looks like a lot of fun," said Harold.

Mr. Ferris nodded. "I suppose it does,

Harold. But the ease with which they ride is hard earned. No one can ride like that without a great deal of practice."

The rest of the circus, including the noisy performance on stage, passed quickly for Jocelyn. She meant to keep her attention on the spectacles before her, but it was impossible from her position to miss seeing the looks that passed between Maria and the tutor. It could not be, thought Jocelyn in consternation, that she was jealous of her sister!

She felt the scarlet flooding her cheeks. How utterly reprehensible. Whatever could have come over her? It was not, she told herself firmly, that she did not want her sister to be happy. It was only that – She was forced to admit that what she wanted was a love like Maria's. And how could she have a love like Maria's when there were no men in her life at the moment except the disdainful, condescending Ashburton? There he was again, intruding into her thoughts!

With a frown Jocelyn decided that, since the disquieting Ashburton continued to invade her thoughts, she might as well give some attention to their problem. How long would it take the Viscount to discover Maria's partiality for Peter Ferris? she wondered. Had she made a mistake in counseling them not to approach Ashburton immediately?

She sighed. There was no way to tell if she had done the right thing. She had been acting on her experiences with other men. There had been no way she could have known that Ashburton was different from the men she had previously dealt with who had been older parental figures, or young exquisites. She had never faced and fought a man like the Viscount; nothing appeared to reach him or ever penetrate the hard shell that encased him.

Tears, a weapon she had not employed against him, would never have worked on a man like Ashburton. Of course, tears were not her method of attack. They were too traditionally feminine and seemed a weak and underhanded way of going about getting something. She preferred a more straightforward approach, fighting him, so to speak, on his own territory. That was how she had faced Ashburton, but it had not worked.

"Jocelyn! Jocelyn!" She realized that Maria was tugging at her arm. "The circus is over, my dear. We're going home now."

"Of course, Maria." Jocelyn flushed again. "I – I was daydreaming."

From that moment until the carriage pulled up in front of the house on St. James's Square, Jocelyn kept her attention rigidly on the chattering boys and the sights of London around them. She would not let the Viscount spoil the pleasure of their outing.

"Oh, Mama!" cried Harold. "This has been the best day of my life!"

"You must thank Mr. Ferris," said Maria. "He planned today's outing."

"Thank you, sir," chorused the boys.

They were still chattering as they hurried up the walk into the house with the adults following them. Jocelyn had herself passed Rears, behind the smiling Maria and Mr. Ferris, into the front hall, when the sudden cessation of noise caused her to pause and look up. There, regarding her with a ferocious glare that made her knees weak, stood the Viscount Ashburton.

Chapter 11

There were several long moments of silence while Jocelyn fought to regain her equilibrium. Then Ashburton spoke. "So," he said with such obvious sarcasm that Jocelyn winced for the boys, "as soon as I absent myself, you go cavorting about the city in this unseemly fashion."

Maria blanched visibly and Peter Ferris frowned. "Boys," he said quietly, "I believe that you had better go to the schoolroom. There are matters there that need your attention."

"Yes, sir," said the boys. "Right away, sir." And they sped silently away, obviously relieved to escape the Viscount's wrath.

"You may go with your charges," the Viscount told Mr. Ferris.

The tutor shook his head. "I think not, milord."

The Viscount raised an eyebrow. "I believe you exceed your place, Ferris."

The tutor's face did not change, even under Ashburton's glare. "Perhaps I do, milord; I do not think so."

"Mr. Ferris!" Maria pleaded, but the tutor shook his head again.

"No. This has gone far enough." He faced his lordship. "I must speak to you, milord; it would be best to do so in private."

"Indeed!" Ashburton seemed to ponder this for a moment. Then he shrugged. "Come with me, all of you. We may as well settle this now."

Jocelyn, watching her sister, moved to take her hand just as Maria took a step toward the tutor. She shook her head slightly. As they followed the men to the library, Jocelyn felt the trembling of Maria's hand in hers. She pressed it reassuringly but she was forced to admit to herself that she, too, was frightened. If Mr. Ferris intended to tell the Viscount about Maria and himself, this interview would be far from pleasant. For a moment she wished that she had never left Sussex, but then she straightened her shoulders. She could not leave them to face his lordship alone, even if she found herself far from ready for battle.

His lordship led the way into the library and turned to Jocelyn. "You will shut the door, Miss Franklin. That should assure us privacy."

Jocelyn bridled, but she did as she was told. There were far more important things at stake here than a triviality like that.

"I suggest that the ladies sit down, milord," said Peter Ferris firmly.

Ashburton gestured imperiously to the divan and Jocelyn settled herself and her sister there. She was glad to have the support of something under her suddenly weak legs. Ashburton was a formidable opponent.

The Viscount turned on Peter Ferris. "Now," he said curtly, "perhaps you will be so kind as to enlighten me concerning this important private business."

The tutor nodded. "First, milord, I wish to say that today's outing was my idea. I thought the boys might enjoy themselves and learn something at the same time."

The Viscount shrugged. "I find nothing wrong with that. I myself enjoyed Astley's as a boy. But the Marchioness and her sister . . ." – his eyes raked Jocelyn – ". . . should not have gone."

Jocelyn felt Maria tremble beside her.

"They should have known better."

"I take the full responsibility for the outing," said Peter Ferris with determination. "Ladies on occasion attend the circus. I saw to it that they were well protected."

The Viscount's frown deepened. "I have no control over the doings of the headstrong and wild Miss Franklin." His eyes swept over her again. "But the Marchioness is my charge. I do not find Astley's a suitable place for her to be seen. However, she is sensible enough to know that. I shall speak to her about it."

The Viscount's tone signified dismissal, but the tutor did not move.

"You may leave us, Mr. Ferris," said the Viscount curtly.

The tutor shook his head. "I have further matters to discuss with you, milord."

"Further matters?" The scowl on Ashburton's face made Jocelyn shrink back on the divan. Peter Ferris was courageous to take on such an adversary.

"Yes, milord."

"Well, then, out with it."

"Since you are milady's guardian, it is to you that I must come. I wish to marry her."

For a long moment his lordship stood staring. "You wish to marry the Marchioness?" he said in unbelieving tones.

"My position in life is unfortunate," Peter Ferris said evenly, "and I will not lie to you about my future. I am not only a younger son; there are three brothers older than I to whom the title would fall should anything happen to the eldest. I have no hope to a title and I have little in the way of fortune. But I am a hard worker and I should always take good care of milady and her sons."

Ashburton took a step toward the tutor and Maria gasped. "You are a fool, Ferris, to think you can get around me with such noble sentiments. You forget I know the value of the lady's holdings. I have dealt with fortune hunters before, you see. Your efforts here are quite useless."

Maria wrenched her hand free of her sister's and was at Peter Ferris' side immediately. Jocelyn watched in amazement as her sister turned on his lordship. "Mr. Ferris is not a fortune hunter!" she cried angrily. "He is a fine, upright man. And – and I shall never marry anyone but him. Never! Do you

154

hear?" Sobbing, Maria rushed from the room. Jocelyn considered following her, but she was loath to leave Mr. Ferris alone with the irate Viscount.

"I understand your lordship's feelings," the tutor said gravely, "and I believe that you genuinely wish the best for milady, as I do myself. I did not intend to form an attachment for her. But, since I have, and she for me, I refuse to desert her. I know that this must seem very sudden. You will need some time to think about it. Therefore, I will leave you now and we can discuss it at a later time after you have had some chance to think."

"No amount of time —" began the Viscount, but Peter Ferris was no longer there to hear him. He had left the library with quiet determination.

He was quite a man, Peter Ferris was, Jocelyn told herself, but then she had no more time for admiration. The Viscount rounded on her. "So! You knew this, I suppose." He glared down at her.

Jocelyn leaped to her feet. "Yes, I knew. I know, too, that it is unusual. But you must see that his love for Maria is real. He is not after her holdings."

The Viscount laughed harshly. "For a woman who purports to know the world, you are incredibly naive. If a man professes love, it means nothing. Love is a delusion. It is an affliction of schoolroom misses and moonlings. Your sister needs a responsible man of –"

"Mr. Ferris *is* a responsible man!" Jocelyn interrupted him without a thought. "He has behaved most admirably."

Ashburton smiled nastily. "He failed in his attempt to win you and so he turned his attentions to your sister."

"Oh!" For a moment Jocelyn's anger rendered her speechless. How utterly dense he could be! "Mr. Ferris never had –" She stopped in mid-sentence, realizing that it would not be wise to tell the Viscount the depth of her sister's devotion to the tutor. A man of Ashburton's suspicious nature could only imagine the worst.

"You are incredible," she said crisply. "Such incredible stupidity I have never before been privileged to observe." She knew that she had reached him when she saw him tense and his brows snap together.

"I fail to see the nature of my stupidity," he replied stiffly. "My major concern has been to see that your sister is safely and properly married. A fortune-hunting tutor is hardly an appropriate choice."

"Oh!" cried Jocelyn again. "You are quite incapable of understanding. Mr. Ferris is a

156

gentleman – a real gentleman in a manner you can never hope to copy."

The Viscount's face darkened perceptibly, but she went on. "Maria genuinely cares for him, and he for her. But you, you high and mighty Lord-know-it-all, you can only scoff at love and devotion. You must put your trust in title and fortune – things quite apart from the man."

She was breathing heavily and she felt an insane desire to pummel him with her fists. "You called Peter Ferris a fool!" she cried. "But it is you who are the fool, who cannot recognize what a priceless treasure such love is."

She was dismayed to find that her voice had broken in the middle of the sentence and that treacherous tears had risen to her eyes. She turned away quickly lest he should see them and laugh at her.

She stood still for a moment, blinking, her eyes too blurred for her to make her way from the room. And then strong hands on her shoulders spun her around. She knew that her cheeks were wet and that tears hung on her lashes, but she was powerless to brush them away.

"Look at me," he said in a strangely gentle tone. Jocelyn raised her eyes to his.

"You speak very fervently in favor of

this delusion love," he told her, his face unreadable but his eyes unusually sympathetic. "You must have a firsthand acquaintance with it to be so knowledgeable about the matter."

Jocelyn shook her head. "I – no, I don't," she admitted, but added, "But that does not blind me to the value of love. If I should be fortunate enough to find such devotion, I should not consider the matter of rank and title or fortune of any regard at all."

For a long moment the Viscount held her blue eyes with his dark ones. Jocelyn found it disquieting, but when she thought of turning away, she seemed strangely unable to do so. Then, while she still was lost in his gaze, he pulled her closer to him. She knew, when he bent his head, that he meant to kiss her. But his grip was firm; she was unable to avoid the mouth that closed over hers.

Jocelyn willed herself to stand quietly, coldly. She would not let the Viscount reach her. She did not yield to the warm pressure of his arms, though she found to her dismay that her flesh wanted to melt against his. The pressure of his mouth on hers was gentle and persistent. A curious warmth began to steal ove her. Jocelyn fought it with all her will, so when his lordship put her away from him, her detachment was still intact.

He gazed down at her stiff face sardonically. "How can you speak of love? You are too frozen even to recognize passion if it should strike you." He shook his head. "Take my advice, Miss Franklin, forget about love. Look instead for a husband who can provide well for you. That is what a sane woman should do."

Jocelyn barely registered his last words; she was consumed with the anger that surfaced in her when he again called her frozen. "I may be frozen for you, milord," she said scathingly. "But you forget. I do not need a husband to provide for me. I am quite capable of doing that for myself." She took a deep breath. "It is only your overweaning arrogance that makes you believe me cold. I assure you that for the right man I should not be."

Ashburton smiled cynically; his dark features seemed harsh. "Your assurances, Miss Franklyn, are of little value to me. If you insist on throwing away your life in the pursuit of will-o'-the-wisps, there is little I can do about it." He frowned. "However, I do deplore the reprehensible effect this type of thinking has on your sister. It greatly compounds the difficulty of my finding a proper husband for her."

Jocelyn's hands clenched into fists but she

managed to speak quietly. "My sister has already found a proper husband – a man she loves and respects. Why don't you let them have their happiness?"

"This so-called happiness is a delusion," repeated Ashburton sternly. "I am here to deal with the reality of the everyday world. I am here to see that your sister is securely provided for."

"Securely imprisoned is what you mean!" flared Jocelyn. "Imprisoned with someone she does not love. Well, Maria will not do it. She may be meek and humble about most things, but she meant what she said. She will marry Peter Ferris – or no one!"

Ashburton glowered. "I am aware that you intend to aid and abet her in this lunacy. I implore you, Miss Franklin, if you have any feeling for your sister, advise her to forget this tutor; advise her to consider the 'real' world."

Jocelyn drew herself to her full height. "I shall never do such a terrible thing. I do wish Maria to consider 'reality,' but it is the reality of love that I wish her to know, not the reality of the *ton* to which you give such misguided allegiance. I will stand with her. She will not give in."

"Do not be too sure of that," replied the Viscount. "I have means at my disposal which can hardly be resisted."

Jocelyn felt a chill go over her. "Surely you would not treat my sister like a schoolroom Miss and confine her to her room on bread and water," she retorted bitterly.

Ashburton smiled harshly. "I am not that sort of man, though considering the difficulty I have encountered in dealing with you, I have a great deal of sympathy for fathers who take recourse to such measures. If I were your father, however, I believe I would have employed even more stringent measures, like a good spanking."

Jocelyn trembled with indignation. "Tonight I shall give thanks that such a horrible fate has been spared me," she said icily. "How fortunate that no woman has agreed to marry you, and you will therefore have no daughters to mistreat."

"You have the thing turned around," declared the Viscount, stung by her suggestion that a woman might reject him.

"Indeed? How so?"

"I have offered for none. I never found one whom I could contemplate being married to."

"How very fortunate for womankind," declared Jocelyn venomously. She was quite beyond any rational thinking, wanting only to hurt this man as he had hurt her.

Ashburton's face darkened. "Do not tempt me too far, Miss Franklin. It may not be too late for you to experience the salutary effects of a spanking."

Jocelyn blanched as he took a threatening step toward her. "You wouldn't," she whispered, her throat gone suddenly dry.

Ashburton's features were saturnine. "Don't push me too far. I have never yet struck a woman, but you are certainly a prime candidate."

"I am a woman, not a child to be spanked," she said, infuriated.

His lordship shook his head. "No, you are not. You are frozen in girlhood, unable to reach the emotions of a woman."

His words struck deep, hurting her. "That's not true," she cried, "just because I do not respond to you! You are not, after all, such a wonderful man."

He took another step closer. Jocelyn felt her breath come faster and her cheeks color up, but she refused to turn tail and run. She could not stand the thought of him laughing at her retreat. It was better to face him down. He was only trying to scare her. He would not dare to act on that threat.

"Perhaps," he said softly, eyeing her consideringly, "I should kiss you until I

melt that frozen woman. I could, you know."
He loomed over her, his power palpable.

Jocelyn refused to lower her eyes. "You
have an unsufferably high opinion of yourself,
milord. If you touch me again I shall scream."

Ashburton smiled, his lips curling
mischievously. "A very feminine reaction."

Jocelyn strove in vain to control her fury.
"You are a bully!" she cried. "A tyrannical
bully! You have everything on your side – the
law, public opinion. I know that, but don't
think I will give in!" she shouted, almost
hysterically.

He grabbed her shoulders and shook her.
"Stop this nonsense immediately. It is
unfortunate that you could not be persuaded
to return to Sussex where your eccentricities
harmed only yourself, but you refused to leave
and so now you must bear your defeat."

Jocelyn glared furiously at him, her blue
eyes sparkling, her head high. "There will be
no defeat, milord, except yours. I will not give
in on this, nor will Maria. Frozen I may be,
but I am very strong."

For a long moment he glared at her
determined and willful face and then he
smiled slowly. "I have never yet lost a
contest to a woman," he said, pulling her
into his arms.

This time as his lips descended, she twisted

163

to avoid them. She could not summon the familiar coldness that had protected her before. She fought him with all her strength, but finally he pinioned her arms against her sides and crushed her to him.

He took her lips savagely, brutally, and her strength seemed gone. Crushed against him, she felt the pounding of his heart against her breast and her mouth, quite against her will, softened and opened under his. She was without will or volition as she lay limply against him, his mouth devouring hers. Her mind seemed to have ceased functioning and strange new sensations raced through her trembling body.

When finally he raised his head, he, too, was breathing heavily. He gazed down at her, his eyes half-lidded. "I knew it," he whispered. "I knew a woman slept within you."

Jocelyn fought to regain her senses. In some terrible way she felt that he had defeated her. In awakening that sleeping woman, he had somehow reached an ally. The thought frightened her.

"I was wrong about one thing, though," he said, his lips caressing the hollow of her throat where her blood pulsed heavily. "You are made for passion. I know that now."

He bent toward her once more and she

was powerless to stop him, powerless to stop herself from responding. Then he was gone, striding from the room without a word and leaving her there, shaken, to face the realization that had just struck her. The intense longing she had felt had not been for a nameless, unknown man. On the contrary, it was Ashburton, the top-lofty, tyrannical, condescending Ashburton, that she wished to have look on her with eyes of love!

With a sob Jocelyn dropped into a chair and buried her face in her hands.

Chapter 12

Somehow Jocelyn forced herself to prepare for the dinner table that night, but it was only because of Maria that she was able to do it. Sheer terror seemed to overcome her at the prospect of meeting Ashburton's knowing eyes. She reached far back into the wardrobe for her oldest, most unfashionable gown, as though wearing it could deny the force of the emotions storming through her, though the painful reflections of the past hour had thoroughly convinced her of the uselessness of trying to deny her feelings. She loved

Ashburton. How it had happened or why it had happened was an utter mystery to her, but the fact itself was inescapable.

If ever Ashburton discovered her secret, if ever he knew how the woman within her longed for his approbation, he would have a formidable weapon to use against her. The thought terrified her. To face his derision or his pity – Jocelyn stifled a sob at the thought. She could never stand to have that awful man know how she felt.

Such stupidity, she told herself firmly. If she had to fall in love at this late date, why could it not be with a man of some sense who at least recognized the existence of love? But no, like some ignorant schoolgirl she had to fall in love with a cynical misogynist who had no desire for a woman in his life.

She stared at herself in the cheval glass. What an utter and absolute mess she had made of this trip to London. The tears threatened to spill from her eyes again and she frowned at herself. She would not appear at the dinner table with red-rimmed eyes. She would not give him that satisfaction. If he ever brought up the subject of his kisses, she would simply inform him that she had decided to let him see that she was *not* frozen. He might not believe her, but if she refused to acknowledge that she was moved by his kisses, he could not know for certain. It was her only defense against him.

She straightened her shoulders and prepared for the ordeal of going downstairs and pretending that nothing at all had happened to her.

She met her sister at the bottom of the stairs. Maria's eyes, slightly red and puffy, indicated that she, too, had spent some time in tears. "Do not worry," said Jocelyn firmly. "He cannot force you to do anything. If nothing else avails, there is always Gretna Green."

"Jocelyn!" Maria's shock was so great that her sister knew she had not even considered that alternative.

"It is an option," Jocelyn declared. "We must not disregard any choices we have."

"But, Jocelyn, the Viscount ... he would –" Maria's imagination seemed to fail her. It was apparent that she could not bring herself to consider the enormity of his lordship's reaction.

Jocelyn shrugged. "He is angry all the time, anyway. You know that. Nothing we can do pleases him." A fleeting memory of the satisfied look on his face after that kiss seared her memory and she all but flinched visibly. "Come, Maria, we are not going to give in. There is no question of that. We will simply stand up for your rights, and if that does not prevail, why, then we shall plan for your elopement." She forced herself to smile. "It might be fun."

Maria attempted to smile in return, but she did not succeed. "I am frightened, Jocelyn, really frightened. Oh, why did he have to come and ruin everything?" Jocelyn shook her head. "There is no use bemoaning our fate. We must simply make our own." She said this somewhat more confidently than she felt it. Most assuredly she had not chosen to fall in love with a man like Ashburton. Had she suspected that such a thing might happen, she would never have stayed.

It was too late for that now. Although she could not stop herself from being attracted to the high-handed Viscount, she could stop herself from giving in to that attraction. She could certainly stop herself from letting that insolent man detect it! If she could not entirely check the force of her emotions, she would at least control them.

She felt her cheeks flush again at the memory of her helplessness in his arms. The arrogant braggart! So he thought that he could bend any woman to his will, did he? Well, he would find out differently. Her body may have betrayed her, but her mind was still working. She would never admit to defeat at his hands, not if she herself had to drive Maria and Mr. Ferris to Scotland!

She would lie, cheat, do whatever was necessary to ensure Maria her love. As for herself, Jocelyn stifled a sigh, there was no future in love for his lordship. Whether she thwarted his plans for Maria or not, he would continue to think of her only as another woman, a creature easy to impress either by scolding or caressing.

This vision of herself made Jocelyn writhe inwardly. Such a man, with no respect for a woman as a human being, was unfit to be a husband. It would be sheer madness for any sensible woman to consider him in that light. Besides, she told herself with a self-mocking fury, his kisses were not evidence of love – or anything else, for that matter. The inflated Viscount used kisses as weapons, and used them unfairly, she thought bitterly.

"Jocelyn, Jocelyn." Maria smiled tenderly. "I fear you are woolgathering again."

Jocelyn sighed. "You are right. I seem to do it quite often lately. Where is Mr. Ferris?"

"He's with the boys," Maria answered. "They are so fond of him."

"I know," replied Jocelyn. "He is an estimable man. You are very fortunate."

"I know, Jocelyn. I know."

Together the sisters moved toward the dining room.

"Mr. Ferris will join us for dinner, won't he?" asked Jocelyn.

"Of course," replied Maria. "He says that not to would be an evidence of fear. And he will not have his lordship believe that he fears him."

Jocelyn nodded. "That is sensible of him. We must never let the Viscount think we are wavering."

The sound of footsteps caused her to turn, but she knew before she raised her eyes to the nonchalant figure that moved so easily toward them that it was the Viscount. "Good evening, ladies," he said, but his casual tone was belied by the intent look he gave her. With great effort she kept her face from betraying the waves of emotion that were coursing through her.

"Good evening, milord," she replied as calmly as she could.

The Viscount's eyes lingered on her face and Jocelyn fought to keep from coloring up.

Then he shifted his gaze to Maria. "Where is Mr. Ferris?"

"Mr. Ferris," said Maria with quiet dignity, "is with the boys. He will be here at any moment." She seemed to brace herself for some further words from the Viscount, but he said nothing more, merely moving toward the French doors to look out into the courtyard.

Jocelyn exchanged a look with her sister and gave her an encouraging smile. Maria returned it tremulously.

Then Peter Ferris entered the dining room. "I am sorry to have kept you waiting, milady," he said.

"We have just gotten here ourselves," Maria hastened to add. "Come, let us eat."

Few words were exchanged during the meal, which seemed to Jocelyn to drag on interminably. She was confused and troubled by the turmoil within her, and was in no condition to make conversation with anyone, let alone with Peter Ferris or the Viscount. She ate slowly and mechanically, not tasting the roast beef or the other dishes that accompanied it. It took all her efforts to remain calm and controlled.

She was aware that she wanted to look at Ashburton, but she steadfastly refused to do so. She kept her attention firmly fixed on her plate.

At the conclusion of the meal, the Viscount pushed back his chair. "I will be out this evening," he said to Maria.

"Yes, milord."

Jocelyn's eyes went to her sister. Maria,

she could see, was striving hard to maintain her dignity.

Without another word the Viscount rose and made his leisurely way to the door. Jocelyn could not help watching; he moved with such consummate grace. Besides, he could not see her watching him when his back was turned.

At the door he paused and without turning remarked, "Hegers and Marston will be calling again tomorrow." Then he was gone and Maria and Mr. Ferris turned questioning eyes to each other.

Suddenly Jocelyn realized what Ashburton had done. He had acted exactly as though Peter had never spoken to him at all! He meant simply to ignore Mr. Ferris' request.

Jocelyn felt the anger rising. "You will just have to refuse them again," she said firmly to her sister. "He cannot force you to marry anyone."

"No, he cannot," agreed Peter Ferris, "but his lordship holds the pursestrings in this house. He can make it difficult for you."

Maria sent her sister a fearful glance and Jocelyn knew that she was thinking of the tutor's wages. "I don't care!" cried Maria, going to Mr. Ferris' side and reaching for his hand. "I don't care what he does. I will marry no one but you!"

Peter Ferris shook his head. "I fear it will not be an easy task."

"Nevertheless, we will do it." Jocelyn kept her voice firm. "I believe I shall retire early tonight. The day has been quite a long one."

"All right, Jocelyn." Maria was still disturbed. "I will see you in the morning." She hesitated. "You will be with me during calling hours?"

Jocelyn nodded. "Of course. Don't worry about that. Good night."

At the door Jocelyn turned back and discovered Maria taking the tutor's arm. She turned away again quickly, angrily aware that her eyes were filling with tears. What a watering pot she was getting to be, she thought bitterly. In the past weeks she had probably shed more tears than in all of her previous lifetime. And to have shed them over such a haughty, arrogant, overbearing tyrant – a man no sensible woman would allow herself to love – made her angrier still.

In her mind she saw herself taking Ashburton's arm and looking up at him. It was surprisingly easy to imagine her own face filled with the kind of radiance that shone from Maria's, but when she tried to imagine an answering look of devotion on the darkly handsome features of the Viscount, she failed. Even in her daydreams, she thought angrily, he scowled at her.

It was with a sigh of relief that she closed the bedroom door behind her. At least she had not run into him in the hall. Now, she told herself sternly, she would dismiss the Viscount from her mind and concentrate on a letter to her steward at Sussex. There were certain projects that she had left in progress and she wished to know their results.

She took out paper, goose quill, and ink and settled herself at the writing desk with determination, but some ten minutes later she realized that the paper before her was still blank. The saturnine face of Ashburton seemed to stare back at her from the page.

If only he loved her, she thought. Then, realizing what she had been wishing, she leaped to her feet and began pacing the room. She must have gone mad, she thought bitterly. By his own admission, a man like his lordship did not "love" anyone. He might desire – she could still feel the heat of his lips on hers – but he did not love. He despised such emotions, considering them delusion.

Jocelyn bit her lip as she paced the floor. The best thing for her to do would be to leave this place. It was dangerous for her to stay in the same house with Ashburton, and very painful. But she could not leave now, when Maria's future was at stake. Her

174

sister would need all the moral support she could get to win out against the Viscount. So, thought Jocelyn, retracing her steps to the writing desk, she had no choice in the matter. She must stay and help Maria.

She picked up the quill and began to write. She would not allow her present lack of control to interfere with the orderly considerations of her life. The floor around the desk gradually grew more and more cluttered with the wrinkled sheets of paper that she discarded, but Jocelyn refused to be deterred and finally she finished a satisfactory letter.

It was with a real sense of accomplishment that she put her seal upon it and then made ready for bed. She grimaced in distaste as she removed the out-of-style gown and slipped on her nightdress. Perhaps it had been a mistake to wear that dress. He might be a bully, but Ashburton knew the ways of women. She may have betrayed her true feelings by choosing that dress.

She raised her hands to her burning cheeks. If he knew, if he ever knew – how he would laugh at her. She could almost see him sneering. She was flooded with humiliation at the thought. Well, there would be no more wearing of old gowns. She would pretend that nothing had changed, that those kisses meant nothing to her. She blew out the candles and crept between the curtains of the great bed.

There was little point in reliving the events of the day. Now that she was aware of the disastrous nature of her feelings about Ashburton, she should be able to deal with him. She must. She would simply dismiss him from her mind. In her memory she returned to the old house in Sussex. She traveled from room to room, recalling every chair, every painting, every item there. But suddenly, as she was recalling the great dining room with its old oak table and chairs, she saw Ashburton, sitting at the head of the table in the place that had been her father's!

A very unladylike expression issued from Jocelyn's lips and she rolled over and punched the pillow. Was there no way to avoid thinking of him? She set her mind on other things, pleasant places she had been, even unpleasant ones. Inevitably, the image of Ashburton intruded, and he always wore the disdainful sneer of the fashionable gentleman and not the smile of devotion that her foolish heart so yearned to see.

"All right, all right," muttered Jocelyn angrily. "I cannot banish him from my mind, so I will think about him. I will think about him till I am sick and tired of the whole miserable business."

She rolled again onto her back and closed her eyes. It took no effort at all to relive the scenes of that afternoon. How long ago it seemed, their cheerful visit to the circus that had ended in such disaster. She relived the scene in which Peter Ferris and Maria had declared their love. Then her memory took her once more through those taunting and bitter moments that she had spent alone with the Viscount. How he had hurt her with his jibes about being a frozen woman. Part of her, she realized, had wished to show him that she was not frozen, that she was quite capable of emotion. But she had not intended to do anything about it. She certainly had not meant to get carried away by her feelings.

Her cheeks burned again at the memory of how his arms had enclosed her, how his lips had claimed hers – and she had submitted! She had acquiesced to his caresses in a way entirely unlike her usual self. Waves of longing had washed over her at his touch, and she had been powerless to stop the response of her body to his.

It shamed her to think that she had fallen for the cheap, shabby tricks of such a man! Perhaps it would have been better to have fled, but the thought of him laughing at her in that sardonic way of his, which he surely would have had she retreated, would have been too much to bear. No, she could not have done that. She had had to stay and face him.

It was far into the night before sleep came to her. When it did come, it was not a restful slumber, but a troubled, turbulent tossing.

Chapter 13

Jocelyn did not see the Viscount when she went down to breakfast the next morning, a circumstance for which she was duly grateful. Maria was sitting at the table and not looking at all cheerful. Jocelyn could see that the irksome task of greeting her two unwanted suitors weighed heavily on her.

That terrible Ashburton – couldn't he see how difficult this was for Maria? She seemed to grow paler every day. Jocelyn sighed. Oh, for the simplicity of her quiet life in Sussex.

The morning passed slowly and Jocelyn wandered from room to room, not knowing what to do with herself, yet impelled by some inner restlessness to keep moving. Maria spent an hour in the schoolroom hearing the boys at their lessons and then emerged looking refreshed and happy.

Too soon for both the sisters, the accepted time for calling came. The Baron had scarcely arrived before the Marquess was announced. Had she been in a better frame of mind, Jocelyn might have found some amusement in the contrast between the two.

In honor of the occasion, the Baron had chosen a bright waistcoat of scarlet silk that did little to hide the girth of his belly, and he topped it by a coat of pale green, popularly called the "parsley mixture." His short, stubby legs were encased in buff-colored breeches and long boots. The whole effect was heightened by his cravat, which was so highly starched as to make it almost impossible for him to turn his head. Against the somber black outfit of the Marquess, the little man appeared startling.

The callers were seated almost across from each other, and Jocelyn was quite amused by the spectacle of the two of them trying to outdo each other in conversation. And then, deserting politeness, the Baron turned to her. "I have visited Lord Corning's house as you suggested. Your father was right. The work is of very high caliber."

Jocelyn smiled. "I am glad you liked it."

The Baron continued to discuss the art of wrought iron, Jocelyn nodding from time to time; it was all that was necessary to keep him happy and talking.

The Marquess, on the other hand, though occasionally making a bland remark to Maria, seemed quite unhappy. From time to time he shifted his gaze from his hostess to Jocelyn and the Baron and then back to Maria, as though he expected her to do something. Maria, however, seemed quite content to let the little Baron chatter. If the Marquess did not like it, thought Jocelyn, she really did not care. He would all the sooner be discouraged.

Finally, to the utter relief of Jocelyn and her sister, the two made their bows and departed, the little Baron pressing Jocelyn's hand warmly before he left. Maria heaved a sigh as the door closed behind them and she and Jocelyn settled back on the divan. "Dear me, Jocelyn, they are so dreadfully dull. Nice enough men," she added with that sweetness so characteristic of her, "but so dreadfully dull."

Jocelyn nodded. "They certainly did not have much to say. The Marquess knows only of the weather and the King's health, and the Baron of wrought iron." She shook her head. "And to think that London is supposed to be exciting."

Maria smiled. "I wish that Mountcastle had moved more in society. I should like to give a little *soirée*, have some of society in so that you might be seen. But Mountcastle refused so many invitations that I do not really know where to begin." A frown puckered Maria's white forehead. "I wish that you could meet some gentlemen. We go out so little; no one even knows that you are here."

Jocelyn laughed. "Really, Maria, dear, I did not come to London for that reason. The years have convinced me that a man such as I wish for does not exist. No, don't worry yourself over me. Once you are safely married I shall go happily back to Sussex and live in peace."

Maria did not quite seem to believe this. "Still," she insisted, "it would be nice if you could be seen."

Jocelyn managed a smile. She certainly could not tell Maria that it didn't matter how many men saw her, or offered for her for that matter; her heart had been given irrevocably to the arrogant Ashburton.

It was almost as though her thought had evoked him, for his voice came to them from the doorway behind them. "Your sister is right," he said. "You should be seen."

Jocelyn, feeling the color flood her cheeks, did not turn to face him. "I am not going to be put on display like some freak in a raree show," she said evenly.

The Viscount strode across the room and

made himself comfortable in a chair across from them. Even in her anger Jocelyn could not help noting the arrogant grace with which he moved or the cat-like way that he stretched his long legs.

"You needn't bristle up at a quite reasonable suggestion," he replied. It seemed to her that his dark eyes were laughing at her.

She would not let him irritate her, she told herself firmly. He could be as obnoxious as he pleased. She would simply remain unimpressed.

"I passed the Baron and the Marquess on the street," observed his lordship. "They did not seem to be in high spirits."

Jocelyn snorted. "I doubt that the Marquess has been in high spirits since he was in leading strings, and certainly his presence did nothing to cheer the Baron."

The Viscount frowned. "Common courtesy –" he began.

"Milord," interrupted Maria. Her color was up and her lip trembled, but she continued to speak. "Both Jocelyn and I are women of good breeding. We would neither of us insult a guest. It is simply that both gentlemen are intolerably dull, and together they do not improve."

The Viscount glanced sharply at Jocelyn. "One would hope that a husband needn't always be witty."

"I should suppose not," replied Jocelyn stiffly. "But he might at least say something worth listening to once every hour or so."

Ashburton scowled. "Perhaps you have forgotten their honorable intentions."

Jocelyn snorted again. "They honor a fortune, you mean. If Maria were penniless, neither one would give her another look."

Ashburton's scowl deepened. "You will get nowhere objecting to custom."

Jocelyn glared at him. "That is what you say. People made the customs and people can change them."

The Viscount shook his head. "You are exceedingly foolish. Your sister needs a husband; here are two fine upright men of honorable character, yet you scoff at them."

Jocelyn straightened her shoulders. "You forget, milord. Maria has made her choice; there is no need for further suitors."

The Viscount ignored this remark and Jocelyn felt her anger rising again. Whatever he did not wish to answer, he just refused to hear.

Ashburton turned to Maria. "It is not a bad idea to go out. I have therefore engaged a box for us at Covent Garden."

Jocelyn was about to make a cutting refusal when she caught the rapt expression on

183

Maria's face. "Oh, I have so wanted to see Kemble in *Macbeth*. And Mrs. Siddons.''

Jocelyn's protest died in her throat. A trip to the theater would obviously be a treat for her sister. The Viscount was just nasty enough to cancel the whole thing if she refused to go, and she had wanted to see *Macbeth*.

Ashburton smiled. "I thought you would enjoy it, and since I knew you had no plans for the evening, I thought we should go tonight.''

"Oh!'' cried Maria. "I must think of what to wear. Come, Jocelyn, we must check the wardrobes immediately.''

"I have taken the liberty of ordering the carriage around for the three of us,'' said his lordship just as they reached the door. "I am dining with my aunts tonight but will return in time for the theater.'' His voice took on the tight quality it always did when he referred to his aunts.

Maria paused as though to say something, but Jocelyn squeezed her hand tightly and hurried her off toward the stairs.

They had reached the landing and were out of hearing distance of Rears when Maria turned tear-filled eyes to her sister. "Mr. Ferris. I didn't think.''

Jocelyn patted her sister's arm. "Mr. Ferris

can go by himself. You can give him the time off to go, and Nurse can watch the boys. Then you will be able to talk about the performance together afterward."

Maria's face brightened, then fell. "But his lordship."

"His lordship has no right to tell you how to treat Mr. Ferris. You are perfectly within your rights to allow him time off."

"If only we might go together," sighed Maria.

Jocelyn swallowed over the lump in her throat. "Someday you shall, Maria, I promise you."

Maria gave her sister a brief hug. "You are such a comfort to me, Jocelyn. I should be lost without you."

"Nonsense," declared Jocelyn stoutly. "You would stand up and fight even if I weren't here. But don't worry, I won't leave until you are Mr. Ferris' wife."

Maria's face brightened at this prospect, and as they considered and rejected several dresses, Jocelyn did her best to keep her sister's spirits up. Mountcastle had rarely taken his young wife into society, and Maria had seldom been to the theater. This evening's performance would be a rare treat for her. Jocelyn wanted to do all she could to make it pleasant.

It was some time later before they finally determined what to wear. It was decided that Maria's blonde beauty would be shown to its best advantage in a white lace over-dress over a pale pink satin slip, gathered high under the bosom with short full sleeves of pink satin slashed with white lace. Her hair was to be arranged in loose ringlets with the back braided in a crown. She decided to wear her diamonds and the long pendant earrings matched with a double strand gleaming at her throat would give her a touch of elegance. She would look quite lovely, Jocelyn was sure.

For Jocelyn, they had decided upon the gown of blue green silk. It was deceptively simple, with a square-cut neck and long sleeves trimmed with gold silk ribbon, with the skirt ending in a deep flounce. The sheer material was almost iridescent. She chose to wear the pearls that had been her mother's – a single strand, but perfectly matched. She would put two matching pearl drops in her ears. She would feel more comfortable wearing the pearls than any of the more expensive jewels that Maria offered her.

"I could never understand why Mountcastle gave me so many jewels," Maria sighed. "We seldom went anywhere. I had no place to wear such things."

Jocelyn smiled. "Men behave strangely at

times, my dear. Perhaps he thought of them as an investment. Jewels are often worth a great deal, and these are exclusively yours." Her eyes lit up. "Maria! The jewels are yours! The Viscount has no say over them!"

Maria looked at her sister in bewilderment.

"Don't you see?" cried Jocelyn. "You may sell them or borrow on them or do anything you please."

Maria frowned. "I do not think that Mountcastle intended –"

"You can't know what he intended," Jocelyn said. "All you have is the fact that the jewels are yours to do with as you please."

Maria's frown did not lighten. "Mr. Ferris –" she began.

"I know," replied Jocelyn impatiently. "Mr. Ferris is an honorable man. Right now you needn't even mention them. They will be your secret store against hard times." They might finance a trip to Gretna Green, thought Jocelyn, though she kept this thought to herself.

As the sisters gazed at the gleaming jewels, Jocelyn found herself wishing that finances were the only problem in their lives. "Come," she said. "Put these away and we shall go tell Mr. Ferris that he is to have the night off – to see *Macbeth*."

"He will be so pleased to go to the theater

again. It's one of his favorite pastimes."

"Then why has he not gone for so long?" inquired Jocelyn as they moved toward the schoolroom.

Maria flushed. "He said he did not wish to go if he could not share it with me, but he will go tonight. He will enjoy it, I'm sure."

They had arrived at the schoolroom door and Maria tapped softly and entered. The boys were sitting at their desks, but it appeared that little schoolwork was being done at the moment. Both boys' eyes were focused on the center of the floor, where Spot and Samson, their teeth clamped on an outgrown shoe, struggled valiantly to wrest it from each other. As the pups growled and braced their little legs, Jocelyn was forced to chuckle. How very ferocious they appeared, battling over that shoe. Their father's blood was certainly evident in them.

The boys looked up. "Hello, Aunt Jocelyn," they chorused. "The pups are playing tug-of-war."

"I see," said Jocelyn with a smile. "Are you sure they know they are *playing?*"

Harold grinned. "Oh, they'll stop if we tell them to. We've been training them."

The pups, sensing that they had lost their audience, dropped the shoe in common accord and scurried to their respective masters. Jocelyn smiled at the expressions of pleasure on the little faces as the boys scratched them in their favorite places. Her gift had been a wise choice.

She saw Maria look toward the tutor and she turned her attention to the boys. Mr. Ferris was a sensitive man. He would be able to reassure Maria.

"Next year," said Jocelyn, "your mother must bring you to Sussex. The country is lovely. We'll have you up on some fine ponies and galloping all about the countryside."

"Oh, Aunt Jocelyn!" cried Tom. "That would be capital. And we can bring the pups, too."

Jocelyn nodded. "Of course. They can see their old home again."

"Aunt Jocelyn?" The younger boy's eyes were wide.

"What is it, Harold?"

"I – I don't know how to ride. I have never learned."

Jocelyn chuckled and reached out to ruffle the boy's hair affectionately. "Don't worry about it, Harold. You have your grandfather's blood in you, and he was the finest horseman in the county. With a little practice you'll do quite well."

The boy's eyes grew even wider. "Oh,

189

Aunt Jocelyn. You're – you're –" Harold seemed unable to find a word that sufficiently expressed his gratitude.

"It's all right, Harold. I understand."

Jocelyn reached out to scratch behind the ears of the bulldog pup that the boy had lifted into his arms. How little it took, she thought, to please the small animal. Attend to his needs and give him attention and he would be happy.

It was only man – that rational animal, as the philosophers called him – who was cursed with thought. Only men and women could think themselves into a condition of misery. Well, thought Jocelyn, stiffening her backbone, she would not do so any longer. She was a sensible and competent human being and she would function like one. There would be no more tears, no more sighing, and no more longing for the impossible.

She looked across the room to see how her sister was faring. Maria was smiling. Peter Ferris was smiling, too, but the marks of strain were apparent around his eyes and a certain tightness showed at his mouth. This uneven struggle with the Viscount had been difficult for the sensitive tutor.

Sensitive people, Jocelyn told herself with some bitterness, did not fare well in this harsh world, especially when they had to contend with the likes of Ashburton. The Viscount was the hardest, most adamant man she had ever encountered. It was incredible how insensitive he could be. She straightened her shoulders. She would not let these thoughts of Ashburton lower her spirits or sap her strength. She intended to fight to the end for Maria's happiness.

Maria and the tutor came toward her. Again Jocelyn noted the glow that came from her sister's face. How could the Viscount fail to see how very much Maria cared for Mr. Ferris and how very good the man was for her? But then, the Viscount seemed not to be aware of – or at least not to care about – anyone else's feelings. Witness his assault on her person!

"Mr. Ferris says it will be a memorable evening," Maria said with a smile. "He will go, too, and see the play from the pit."

"That sounds like an excellent idea." Jocelyn smiled at the two of them, ignoring the burst of pain in her heart. In spite of all their problems, Maria and Mr. Ferris had the look of happiness of those who are secure in their love. It was a look Jocelyn never expected to wear.

Chapter 14

After dinner, a pleasant relaxed meal, since Ashburton was not at the table, Jocelyn put on the blue-green muslin with its white satin slip. As the sheer material fell over her head, she marveled again at the fineness of the texture and the excellent work of the dressmaker. The gown's classically simple lines complimented her slender figure and the color echoed her eyes. She let Maria's dresser arrange her hair in a mass of supposedly unruly curls in the front with the rest pulled back and coiled with a gold silk ribbon running through. The dresser called it *à l'antique* and Jocelyn's lip curled somewhat disdainfully as she considered how much time was devoted to such deceptions by the fashionable ladies of the *ton*. Still, she sat quietly until the dresser pronounced herself satisfied with her handiwork.

After the woman had hurried to do Maria, Jocelyn examined herself critically in the cheval glass. She did not look like she was at her last prayers, at least not yet. Her cheeks were flushed and she looked vibrant – whether at the prospect of an evening at the theater or of being with his lordship, she could not really say.

She certainly was looking forward to seeing the great Kemble play the role of Macbeth. Mrs. Siddons was well spoken of in the part of Lady Macbeth, but would just the prospect of an evening at the theater put such sparkle in her eyes and make her somewhat breathless with apprehension? It had never affected her in this fashion before.

Restlessly, she turned away from the glass. This kind of thinking was sheer stupidity. She must discipline herself. The Viscount was to be regarded as an enemy to both Maria and Mr. Ferris and their future together, but even more so as an enemy to herself.

Angrily she snatched up a cashmere and her white kid gloves and made her way toward the door. She did not want to have Ashburton for an enemy, but she had no choice. Besides, she told herself bitterly, even if there were no contention over Maria's future, she could never expect to deal well with the Viscount. He was too domineering, too intent on having his own way in everything. Though she had to respect him for doing what he believed was right, that was not enough. Clashes between them would be inevitable.

But then they would not clash for long, not after Maria's marriage. After that happy event took place, Jocelyn told herself sternly, she would leave immediately for Sussex. It might be difficult getting used to the country again, but she would manage; she must.

When she descended the stairs, she found Maria in the library, looking elegant, but nervous. "Oh, Jocelyn, I am all a-twitter. I haven't been out in so terribly long. Everyone will be staring." She was twisting a handkerchief nervously in her hands.

"Now, Maria, don't upset yourself. They will not be staring at you. And remember, it doesn't really matter what the *ton* think. They are only people."

"Yes, you are correct." The slightly pained expression on Maria's face softened a little.

Jocelyn was searching in her mind for words of reassurance, but a sudden knocking on the front door announced the arrival of Ashburton. The sisters exchanged glances and smiled at each other encouragingly.

Jocelyn realized that she was frightened, too, but it was not the eyes of the *ton* that she feared. She could easily ignore the ogling of young bucks. But the arrogant look that she so often saw in Ashburton's eyes when he regarded her would not be so easy to ignore. It disabled her in some way and made it difficult for her to think properly. Now she must face that look and deal with his lordship for a whole evening. She was thankful that Maria would be there. The prospect of an entire evening alone with Ashburton would have reduced her to a trembling wreck.

The sisters moved toward the hall, where his lordship could be heard in conversation with Rears. As Jocelyn's eyes swept over the Viscount's lean figure, she felt her heart contract. In his coat of blue superfine with gilt buttons, waistcoat of white marcella, breeches of white kerseymore, buckled shoes, and *chapeau bras*, he was a handsome figure, with a lithe grace that marked his every movement.

He turned and found her eyes focused on him. To her annoyance she flushed, but she refused to drop her eyes. she would not allow the man to cow her. "Good evening, your lordship."

Ashburton bowed. "Good evening, ladies. I see that you are on time. Quite admirable."

There was no hint of sarcasm in his voice, and his look as he regarded them both was frankly approving. "You are both looking lovely this evening. I shall be the envy of every man of taste."

Maria smiled nervously. "Thank you, milord. I find that I am a little disconcerted by the prospect of being again in society."

The Viscount smiled, a charming, friendly smile that lit up his dark eyes and gave a brief glimpse of a different sort of man. Jocelyn realized with a start that she had never seen him smile unaffectedly. It gave him an entirely different look, and she thought with a pang that this perhaps was the man who the ladies of the *ton* saw, not the angry one who so often confronted her.

"You need have no fear, milady," he told Maria. "You look quite lovely."

Maria flushed, a procedure which only added to her charm, Jocelyn thought. Then her thoughts left Maria entirely, for his lordship's dark eyes had caught hers and the resulting turmoil inside threatened to overcome her. She managed to remain calm and keep from betraying herself as his lordship asked, "Are you both ready?"

"Yes, milord." Jocelyn forced herself to speak evenly. She could not let him guess her secret.

"Good. I believe I hear the carriage pulling up." He extended a hand for Maria's cashmere.

As she watched the Viscount expertly shawl her sister, Jocelyn engaged in a silent battle with herself. She could put on her own shawl and avoid having Ashburton in such close proximity. But if she did so, he might easily guess her intent and then she would be forced to bear the mockery in his eyes.

But if she did not, if she waited to let him shawl her, she would find the act disturbing. To have him so close to her seemed to induce a paralysis of her will. It would be difficult to keep from him the knowledge of his effect upon her.

The debate was still unresolved when the Viscount turned and took her shawl from over her arm. He looked down at her through dark lashes, his eyes fathomless, not mocking but considering, almost cautious. Then he laid the shawl around her shoulders, carefully adjusting it. He was already gloved, but even so, Jocelyn felt a quiver that went racing down her spine at the touch of his fingers on her back. With iron will, she remained motionless.

Carefully she pulled on her white kid gloves, grateful to have something legitimate to occupy herself with. At that moment she did not think that she could bear to meet his eyes. Her own might reveal too much.

His lordship offered them each an arm and Jocelyn found herself thinking how completely charming the man could be.

It appeared that the Viscount intended to maintain his pose, or whatever it was, through the entire evening. Certainly on the way to Covent Garden he exerted himself to be as pleasant as possible, and Jocelyn found herself responding. At first this realization annoyed her, but a little reflection soon brought her to the conclusion that there was no point in renewing their warfare, at least not at the present moment. If his lordship wanted a truce, he should have a truce. He would not, however, she told herself firmly, find that this evening's entertainment had any effect on their determination. If this were his hope, he was doomed to disappointment, thought Jocelyn with an inner smile. But at any rate, since there obviously was a truce, the sensible thing to do was to enjoy it.

The streets of London were far from deserted. Carriages passed busily to and fro and people crowded the walks. His lordship turned toward her with a winning smile. "I had thought to go in by the Covent Garden entrance. The Grecian architecture there is something to see, especially the columns. I believe one of our critics has said, and rightly, that the whole 'astonishes by its inutility.' The crush tonight, though, would not allow you to get a very good look at it, nor, I judge, at the bas-reliefs illustrating the fathers of ancient and modern poetry. The south side of the portico is devoted to Shakespeare."

Jocelyn smiled at him. "I believe I prefer another entrance," she said, "if we can enter there with less danger of crush."

"I, too, would prefer fewer people," said Maria nervously.

"Well," replied the Viscount, "we shall try the entrance under the Bow Street portico. The crowd may be less dense there."

"Thank you, milord," replied Jocelyn.

As the carriage pulled up to the portico, Jocelyn looked out the window again. Certainly the crush was bad enough even here. Everywhere she looked were ladies in resplendent gowns, shimmering with the finest and most costly jewels, and lords and officers, almost as colorful in their dress clothes or uniforms.

Jocelyn's hand went automatically to the pearls at her throat. Perhaps she would have been better advised to borrow some jewels from Maria when she had offered them. She must certainly appear very plain amongst all these dazzling beauties. Then her chin went up; it didn't really matter. No one would be looking at her tonight, anyway, and she didn't care about the *ton's* opinion.

She caught herself stealing a glance at the Viscount and quickly looked away. It really didn't matter to her what anyone else thought. The swells and the dandies could saunter up and down the pit all they pleased ogling the ladies; they would not bother

her. It was in the eyes of the Viscount Ashburton that she had hoped to appear beautiful, she realized with some dismay, and that was a futile hope. Surrounded by all these lovely young things with eyes only for him, how could she hope to appear beautiful? She was unaware of what an enchanting picture she presented, her dress glimmering in the lamplight, her head high, apprehension and anticipation lending sparkle to her eyes and color to her cheeks.

The Viscount handed them both down from the carriage and gave the driver instructions. Then he turned to her and Maria. "This way, ladies," he said with a charming smile.

Clinging to his arms, Jocelyn and Maria made their way into the theater and up the grand staircase to the boxes, where the sisters were carefully seated by Ashburton, one on either side of him.

Jocelyn looked out over the throng, knowing that Maria was doing the same. Her sister, of course, was seeking the familiar figure of Mr. Ferris, but Jocelyn had other motives. She must do something to keep her eyes away from the darkly handsome man beside her. She was extremely conscious of his nearness, so much so that she found some difficulty in breathing properly. She chastised herself severely; she could not afford to give

200

Ashburton any inkling of the true nature of her feelings.

She kept her eyes upon the crowd below. There seemed to be an abundance of fops in the pit – some strolled up and down the aisles, calling witticisms to each other; some stood chatting and displaying their finery; others were busy ogling the women in the boxes.

Jocelyn found herself the focus of more than one pair of masculine eyes. Several rather inane looking bucks she stared down quite easily. She knew that she was quite adept at injecting scorn into her expression. But one man, dark-haired, who bore a slight resemblance to the Viscount, would not be stared down. Insolently, he kept his eyes fastened upon her.

Jocelyn felt herself coloring up and shifted uncomfortably in her chair. Suddenly the buck himself colored and hastily lowered his eyes. In surprise Jocelyn turned to discover that Ashburton's dark eyebrows had drawn together in a ferocious scowl. It was he who had stared down the offending buck. "Thank you, milord," she murmured without thinking and was surprised to have him swing around and give her a stern look.

"When I am with a woman, I do not appreciate having some fresh young buck make a nuisance of himself."

Jocelyn frowned. "I see, milord. It is a matter of pride with you." Her voice revealed more bitterness than she had meant it to – perhaps because she had experienced a brief moment of joy when it had seemed he had cared for her feelings.

The Viscount seemed surprised. "I suppose you might call it that," he said slowly.

Jocelyn bit her bottom lip and forced herself to remain silent. If she said anymore, she might well give herself away. For a moment she had felt that the Viscount had some concern for her. How foolish, she told herself, to believe something like that of a man of Ashburton's sort. The partiality she had formed for him had definitely impaired her understanding. She would have to get Maria and Mr. Ferris married as soon as possible so she could go back to Sussex and lead a normal life.

As the great curtains opened and the noise in the theater lessened somewhat, Jocelyn cast one more look over the pit, but Mr. Ferris, thankfully, was not in sight. Then she eagerly turned her eyes toward the stage. She had, after all, come to Covent Garden to see the great Kemble and Mrs. Siddons do *Macbeth*, and now the play was beginning.

Kemble seemed to have lost a little stature since her visit to the city for her coming out.

But four years was a long time, and he had not been a young man then. Still, his voice rang out through the theater in truly tragic tones and his gestures were as dramatic as ever.

But it was Mrs. Siddons who really captured Jocelyn's attention. How majestically the actress moved. And when she repeatedly tried to wash the blood of the dead king from already clean hands, Jocelyn felt the gooseflesh rising on her arms. Surely the effects of a guilty conscience had never been more cogently portrayed.

The play entirely captured her attention, so much so that even the disturbing proximity of Ashburton was momentarily forgotten. Of course, during the intermission she was terribly conscious of his presence, but she managed to chat amiably, to respond to him as though he were any beau intent on showing her a pleasant evening at the theater.

She was very much aware, however, that in those days of her coming out her eyes had not sparkled, nor her stomach fluttered because of the presence of any beau. No, in those days she had found all her suitors insipid weaklings who could be wrapped around her finger. They were pleasant enough as toys for an idle moment, but as prospective partners for a lifetime Jocelyn could only have done as she had and refused their flowery offers.

Now she loved a man whom she could not sway, and not only that – he was her sworn enemy and could never be otherwise. She was determined that Maria should be allowed her happiness with Peter Ferris, and his lordship was equally determined that she should not be. Whichever of them won, the result could not lead to any understanding between the two of them.

Maria, Jocelyn noted uneasily, kept scanning the crowd for a glimpse of her beloved Mr. Ferris. Jocelyn frowned. If the Viscount learned that Mr. Ferris was in the audience, he might well be annoyed by it.

In just a few days Maria would be giving Mr. Ferris the quarterly wage that Jocelyn had provided. Of course, Mr. Ferris was not to know that. She could only hope that the Viscount would not see fit to discuss it with the tutor. Peter Ferris was a proud man, and if he knew that his wage had come from Jocelyn's funds – Well, it would certainly be better for all concerned if that did not happen!

Jocelyn tried to catch Maria's eye. There was no need to aggravate his lordship unnecessarily. But her effort was in vain.

Ashburton turned to Maria. "Do you expect to see an old friend?" he asked politely.

Maria shook her head. "Oh, no, milord,"

she faltered. Her cheeks were flaming. "I – I –"

"She simply likes to look at the fashions," Jocelyn interrupted. "You forget, milord. We women are creatures of habit. We must needs see the latest in styles to tell if we are adequately dressed ourselves. Oh, see, Maria, the beautiful redhead in the gown of cream satin. How little jewelry she wears, yet how exquisite she looks."

"I see her," agreed Maria. "She has a great many beaux, too."

"Indeed, she does," agreed Jocelyn, daring to raise her eyes to his lordship's face. What she saw there made her blanch. He was scowling at her ferociously.

"I hardly think that a *lady* would wish to take her standard of fashion from London's leading incognita," he said harshly.

Jocelyn felt the color flood her cheeks, but she refused to drop her eyes. "As I said, milord, we have not been about for some time. And being *ladies*, we are not so apt to recognize an incognita as a *gentleman* might."

The Viscount received this information in silence, but threw her an annoyed glance, his eyes hooded, his dark brows nearly meeting over his nose.

"What has happened to your pose of the charmer?" Jocelyn asked briskly, causing

Maria to gasp aloud. "Is a simple mistake by two ladies sufficient to reduce you to your usual antagonistic self?"

The Viscount coughed suddenly, a rather strangled sound that seemed almost like a laugh cut short. Jocelyn, looking at him in amazement, thought she must be imagining things.

"I regret that I forgot the place of a gentleman," he said to Maria with a smothered smile. "But you must admit that sometimes your sister can be very trying."

Maria had been listening to him politely, but she bridled at his last words. "I admit no such thing, milord," she said firmly. "I have never found Jocelyn a trying person." She assumed an air of injured dignity.

If only she would maintain that, Jocelyn thought, with an inner smile, and not keep looking around the theater for Mr. Ferris. But her hopes were short-lived. Maria's face brightened as she finally spotted the tutor in the crowd.

She did not wave or even recognize him with a nod, yet Jocelyn knew that his lordship had witnessed the interchange. He turned to her and whispered, "It is too bad your sister hasn't your subtlety. But she is too much of an innocent to hide her feelings."

"My sister is entitled to those feelings." Jocelyn spoke softly but with conviction.

The Viscount's lip curled in derision. "A Marchioness does not form an attachment to a tutor. It simply is not done."

Jocelyn tilted her head back and regarded him scornfully. "What a ninny you are. Feelings of partiality know no rank. They are above such things."

"Rather say below," replied his lordship somewhat grimly. "The man has worked upon her emotions. But she will forget him soon enough when he is gone."

"I think not," returned Jocelyn.

Ashburton ignored her and said complacently, "When he discovers that no wage awaits him, he will soon take himself off in search of another position. Then she will forget him."

Jocelyn shook her head. "You do not know women very well," she said, "or you would not suppose such a foolish thing. Maria will never forget Mr. Ferris, no more than I would once forget the man to whom I had given my heart."

The Viscount eyed her skeptically and said with an edge to his voice, "From your behavior I did not suppose that you possessed such an organ."

Jocelyn's hands curled into fists, but she

turned a composed face to him and said in dulcet tones, "Indeed, milord, I fear you are misinformed about a great many things, particularly in regard to me."

She turned her eyes back toward the crowd, but not before she had a glimpse of the thunderous expression on his face. He looked very much as though he'd like to shake her. It was fortunate, she thought bitterly, that they were surrounded by the eyes of the *ton*. That would keep his lordship in line when nothing else would!

Chapter 15

Jocelyn awoke the next morning with a feeling of gloom. As she lay staring up at the curtains that surrounded the bed, she sighed. Last evening with Ashburton had been difficult. Even the pleasant moments had not been easy, and it was painful to recognize that the two of them just did not seem capable of being together without coming to cuffs.

She sighed again. There was no avoiding it. She must get up from this bed and make herself presentable. Another day must be faced. No matter that she did not want to face it. There was no escape from the Viscount and her conflicting feelings toward him.

She dragged herself from the bed, feeling much older than her two and twenty years, and rang for the dresser. She hoped that by the time she went downstairs his lordship would be gone from the house. She really did not know if she could face him again. But she must, she told herself crossly. She could scarcely hide in her bedroom all day. Such a thing would be entirely foreign to her nature.

So, some time later, clad in one of her new morning gowns of yellow jaconet with a full skirt and long loose sleeves, her hair arranged simply in a coil, she made her way down the staircase, determined to present an ordinary face to the world. She met Maria at the foot of the stairs and had just turned to speak to her when a deep masculine voice boomed throughout the great hall. "By Jupiter, this is unpardonable!"

Maria and Jocelyn exchanged worried looks and, lifting their skirts, hurried back up the staircase.

Thundering curses resounded through the upstairs hall. "Milord!" cried Maria, hurrying toward the sound. "Milord, what is it?"

The Viscount loomed large, glaring down at the boys. Tom and Harold were obviously trembling, but they stood their ground and behind them cowered two thoroughly frightened puppies, their vestiges of tails quivering between their legs.

"Milord," repeated Maria, "what ever is the matter?"

Ashburton turned scowling eyes on them and lifted a cravat – or what had once been a cravat. Now it more nearly resembled a beggar's rag. "This!" said his lordship severely. "This is the matter!"

"Oh! Milord!" Maria turned to the children. "Boys, what has happened here?"

Tom stepped manfully forward. "It was my fault, Mama. I left the door open and the puppies got out. His lordship's door must have been open, too. And they got his cravat and were playing with it. You know how they like to play."

Tom's voice threatened to break, but he managed to finish his speech without any unmanly tears.

"Oh, dear, we are so sorry, milord!" cried Maria, her hands fluttering helplessly in the air.

"I should think so," declared the Viscount curtly. "Those dogs have no business being in the house. The creatures will destroy everything."

The boys paled visibly at this.

Jocelyn, who had been watching the whole

scene with something close to amusement, now waited for Maria to come to their aid, but her sister remained helplessly silent, unshed tears glimmering in her eyes.

The situation was no longer humorous. It was senseless for him to frighten the boys so; both of them were close to tears and Jocelyn grew angry. "Really, milord," she said, fixing him with a stern eye, "don't you think that all this is a little excessive? After all, for a mere cravat?"

Ashburton scowled at her. "It is not a question of a cravat. It's the principle of the thing. A man's possessions –"

Jocelyn's patience was exhausted. "Boys, go to your room," she ordered.

"Yes, Aunt Jocelyn," Tom replied, and they left as quickly as they could, the pups in their arms.

"I am most sorry, milord. Really I am," Maria apologized.

"Maria, please go tend the boys." With great control Jocelyn managed to keep her voice kind and firm.

"Yes, of course." And with a last pleading look at her sister, Maria scurried away.

Ashburton scowled at Jocelyn. "You seem to have taken a great deal upon yourself," he commented caustically.

Jocelyn glared at him. "I? What about you?

Thundering about as if a chewed cravat were the end of the world."

"As I have already observed," he began, "a man's possessions –"

"Nonsense!" snapped Jocelyn, perversely pleased to see his face darken further. "Possessions are only that. Surely a man in your position can afford to replace a cravat." She looked up at him, an inquiring lift to her brow.

He looked at her bitterly. "Of course I can. It is a matter of principle." He accented the last word as though this would surely convince her.

Jocelyn dismissed this with an airy gesture. "Principle is all well and good, milord. But what about the boys?"

"What about them?" demanded Ashburton. "They should not have their pets in the house. They are not being properly raised."

"That," cried Jocelyn, her anger aroused, "is untrue! They are fine boys. Didn't you notice how Tom stepped up and took the blame?"

The Viscount's scowl deepened. "There was little sense in his trying to evade it." He cast another look of disgust at the ragged cravat and turned on his heel.

"Milord!" Jocelyn's voice was much shriller

than she had intended, but she forced herself to remain calm.

"What is it now?" asked the Viscount, swinging around to face her.

"Were you never a child?" she asked bitterly. "Were you *born* a tyrant?"

Ashburton's eyes flashed at her. "Of course I was a child," he growled.

"And were you never in any mischief?" she asked, holding his gaze.

The Viscount frowned and looked away. "Of course I was."

"Then I suggest that you recall some of those times."

His scowl did not lighten, but his eyes were thoughtful. "I suppose that now you expect an apology."

Jocelyn smiled sweetly. "That would certainly be the gentlemanly thing to do."

He returned her smile with a grim one of his own. "I must thank you, Miss Franklin, for recalling me to my position as a guest in this household. I have on occasion an abominable temper."

Though the words were obviously those of apology, his expression was far from apologetic. Jocelyn found herself unable to keep from remarking, "I have witnessed that abominable temper on more than one occasion. Have you ever considered that

213

it might behoove you to control it?" she questioned tartly.

Ashburton seemed startled. "Abominable tempers run in my family," he said, as if that explained everything. "Every Ashburton has inherited such a temper."

"Balderdash!" Jocelyn scoffed. "You mean every Ashburton has wanted to have his own way and used this so-called inheritance to get it!"

Ashburton's eyes danced wickedly. "And how do you get what *you* want?" he asked.

Jocelyn caught her breath. "The first thing I had to learn – since I was a woman and not a lord – was that I could not always have what I wanted."

The Viscount shook his head. "That is a lesson lords seldom learn. Indeed, of what use is it to be a lord if one does not take advantage of one's prerogative?" He looked at her consideringly.

Jocelyn shook her head, her curls dancing, and said with some heat, "There are such things as responsibility. *Noblesse oblige.* A lord need not indulge his every whim regardless of the consequences."

The Viscount's eyes narrowed. "In this day and age such a man would be an exception."

Jocelyn shrugged. She knew she was playing with fire, but could not help

214

continuing. "Perhaps, but exceptions are often so much more interesting than run-of-the-mill swells who *think* they know everything."

"If it is your intention to further antagonize me by calling me a swell who knows *nothing*," he said wickedly, "I feel I must caution you. I have been on the town for many years, and that experience has taught me *something*."

His eyes traveled over her in a way that caused her knees to tremble. Still, she forced herself to face him. "You are an abominable man," she declared hotly. "Have you no sense of honor?"

Ashburton raised a devilish eyebrow. "Honor, Miss Franklin? Why should you expect to find such an attribute in a reprobate like me? Indeed –"

He took a step closer to her and it was only by digging her nails into her palms to steady herself that she managed to hold her ground. Jocelyn took a deep breath. His face was so close to hers that the trembling in her knees threatened to spread over her whole body.

"I think," said his lordship softly, his eyes lingering on her face, her lips, "anger serves to melt the part of you that is habitually frozen."

"Milord!" Jocelyn sought about in her mind for something sharp to say, but could

215

find nothing. His nearness quite unnerved her and she grew conscious of the rapid rise and fall of her breasts. Desperately, she dredged her mind for some caustic cut, but it remained a blank. It was as though his eyes, so sharp and penetrating, held her captive in some way. Her breath came faster, but she was unable to turn from his eyes.

He reached out and drew her close. "I have been thinking about that woman that I awakened," he said softly against her hair. "I wish to see if she really exists, or if I only imagined her."

"Milo —" Jocelyn's protest was cut off as he covered her mouth with his. She knew instantly that she could not withstand him. Under the persuasion of his lips, her mouth softened and opened. She felt her body melt against his as he drew her even closer.

For a long moment he kept her in that embrace, his kisses slow and passionate, and Jocelyn, her blood ringing in her ears, could only wish that she might stay so forever.

But finally he put her from him. He looked somewhat bewildered at first, but then smiled triumphantly. "I was right," he said with satisfaction.

Jocelyn was swept from rosy happiness to a sudden blinding rage. So! That was all she meant to him. Another conquest. Another foolish woman mastered by a kiss!

She drew on all her resources to answer him, and when she did she was pleased at how even her voice remained. "I hate to deprive your lordship of such a triumph. But I must remind you that I am two and twenty and, as you have so kindly pointed out, not exactly ugly. It stands to reason, does it not, that I have been kissed on previous occasions? I am not quite a schoolroom Miss."

The Viscount's face darkened perceptibly at her words, his eyes cold and withdrawn. "I congratulate you on your past experience," he said curtly. "What a pity that the man who first awakened that woman did not make her his." Then he spun on his heel and was gone, moving with great angry strides to his chamber and closing the door with a thud that echoed in her heart.

If only he knew, she thought as her eyes filled with tears. If only she did not have to protect herself, could admit to him the truth of his statement – that he was that man and she was his, though he did not want her. She managed to return to her room. It was impossible to go down to breakfast with tears brimming in her eyes. She would never give him the satisfaction of knowing that he had brought her to tears.

Finally, with great effort, she forced herself

to be calm. She bathed her eyes with cold water, and then, looking reasonably normal, she made her way downstairs.

She found that she kept looking around her, wondering if his lordship would come suddenly upon her. But she reached the downstairs without mishap and found Maria in the breakfast room, looking very young and demure in a pale pink sprig muslin morning dres.

"Oh, Jocelyn!" her sister cried. "Whatever did you say to his lordship?"

"I gave him some sound advice," said Jocelyn sternly, glad to pretend that nothing untoward had occurred. "Why?"

Maria flushed. "He came to me and apologized for being so angry. He said that he is unused to dealing with women and children."

Jocelyn felt a moment of pleasure. He was actually capable of hearing what she told him, of realizing that he could make a mistake. "I am pleased for you, Maria. Perhaps that means he will learn to accept Mr. Ferris."

Maria's eyes were bright. "I hope so, Jocelyn. But I almost dare not hope." She wrung her hands. "Every day it seems less and less likely that Mr. Ferris and I will be able to wed." Her voice dropped to a conspiratorial whisper. "And if he ever discovers that his wages came from *your* pocket –"

Jocelyn squeezed her sister's hand. "Don't fret yourself over that, my dear. Just be patient and do not give up on what you want."

"Yes, Jocelyn, I will. But I am still frightened. His lordship has gone out, but he said that he wishes to speak to me privately before dinner. What can he mean to say?"

Jocelyn gave her sister a hug. "There is no way to tell. It's probably some small thing to do with the running of the household. You know how picky he is about such things."

Maria nodded. "Yes, he is rather –" She seemed to be casting about in her mind for some kinder word.

"Come, Maria," Jocelyn urged. "He *is* picky about little things. Do not always be trying to defend him."

Maria smiled sheepishly. "Yes, Jocelyn, I know. But it really must be trying for such a man, unaccustomed to caring for women and children, to be burdened by such a responsibility."

"He is not responsible for *me*," said Jocelyn, quelling her feelings. Then she added, "But I suppose that these circumstances may be unusual for him."

As Maria left her to her chocolate, Jocelyn began to consider his lordship's previous life. Had other women, she wondered, been the recipients of his kisses? Had he awakened others with that mouth that had so undermined her barriers and devastated her senses?

He probably had – and Jocelyn, finding her appetite vanished, left her chocolate half-finished and her scone untouched. She must do something with herself, she thought uneasily as she climbed the great staircase. Perhaps another shopping trip. After all, she needn't purchase much. She would get the little maid Rose to accompany her. To get out of this house would be a distraction, and a sorely needed one.

Chapter 16

When Jocelyn returned to the house on St. James's Square later in the day, Rose, at least, was in high spirits. The little maid did not often get into the fascinating world, and the contents of the shops had made her eyes wide and her cheeks rosy. If only, Jocelyn thought, she herself could still enjoy such simple pleasures.

But all pleasure seemed to be gone from her

life. When she was not miserable because of an altercation with his lordship or concern for Maria's happiness, she existed in a kind of blankness. Her future stretched before her quite bereft and desolate. Nevertheless, she thought as she made her way to the house, she must keep up at least a façade of normalcy. Maria must never know that her happiness with Mr. Ferris would mean the end of any chance Jocelyn might have with the Viscount. And, of course, she reminded herself grimly, Ashburton had no partiality for her. But the gentle Maria would not see that. If she knew, she would worry herself into useless sacrifice. There was little sense in both sisters being unhappy, thought Jocelyn bitterly.

She put on a determined smile as she approached the front door, but it vanished the moment she saw her sister's stricken face. "Take these packages to my room, Rose, and put them away," she said evenly.

"Yes, Miss."

Jocelyn put a hand on her sister's arm and guided her into the library. "Maria, my dear, what is it?"

Maria's perilous composure broke and it was some moments before Jocelyn could get her to stem the flood of tears.

"It's – it's his lordship. He returned." Maria dabbed at her eyes with the lace-edged handkerchief that Jocelyn had put into her hand. "He called me in here. And he said – He said –"

The tears threatened to choke her again, but Jocelyn waited patiently.

"He said that Mr. Ferris must go, that I cannot continue to feed him. He said – he could not understand why Peter persisted in staying where he wasn't wanted."

"Did you tell him –" Jocelyn began.

Maria shook her head. "I didn't tell him why Peter stayed, about your paying his wages, but he said he'd talk to Peter." Maria dissolved into tears again.

Jocelyn was again forced to wait until her sister could control her sobs. "Then what happened?" she prompted.

"He dismissed me and he sent for Peter. Oh, Jocelyn! When Peter came out, he was so white and grim. He walked right past me without a word, without a sign, and he took his coat and hat and left. Oh, Jocelyn, what am I to do?"

Jocelyn gathered her sister in her arms. There was scant comfort she could give her. If the gentle Mr. Ferris had behaved like that toward her, there was no telling what his lordship had said to him.

"Maria, my dear," she said finally, "why don't you go up and lie upon your bed for

222

a while? I'll get Rose to attend to you. Do not worry about Mr. Ferris. I am quite sure he will return. He loves you a great deal, you know."

Maria seemed to brighten a little at this reminder. "Yes, Jocelyn, you are right. Peter will come back. I know he will."

Jocelyn accompanied her sister to the hall and watched her ascend the steps. Then she turned to the butler. "Rears, send someone to find Rose. She should be in my room. Have her attend milady."

"Yes, Miss."

"Where is his lordship?"

"I believe he's in the drawing room, Miss." The butler's dignified expression seemed to unbend a little.

"Thank you," replied Jocelyn crisply. "I wish to speak to him. Please see that we are not disturbed."

"Yes, Miss. I will, Miss." The butler's face almost broke into a smile.

The servants, thought Jocelyn, or at least Rears, would be pleased to have his high-and-mighty lordship get his come-uppance. Straightening her shoulders with determination, she made her way toward the drawing room. At the door she paused momentarily, aware that her knees had begun to tremble.

He was standing with his back to the door. Her heart lurched as her eyes came to rest on the broad shoulders that stretched taut his coat of blue superfine. If only things had been different. If only – She brought herself to an abrupt halt. Such thinking would get her nowhere. She took a deep breath. "Milord?"

He turned to face her, his eyes cold and distant. Almost as though he knew her errand, he spoke. "Ah, Miss Franklin, I have been expecting you."

"Indeed," she contented herself with replying.

"Won't you come in and make yourself comfortable?" he asked with exaggerated politeness, his expression sardonic.

"Thank you." She entered the room and took a seat near him. She settled herself as comfortably as possible under the circumstances.

The Viscount did not wait for her to begin. "I suppose you have come to expostulate with me over my reprehensible behavior," he said evenly.

"Precisely so," replied Jocelyn, feeling as though someone had suddenly struck her a blow in the stomach. He seemed always one step ahead of her.

"I assure you," continued his lordship dryly, "there is nothing you can say to me that will make me change my mind. I have only done what had to be done."

Jocelyn, whose temper had been steadily mounting, fought to control her voice. "You are very sure of yourself," she said, her face pale, her blue eyes like a wall of ice.

"I do what I think best," declared Ashburton stiffly.

"Oh, yes, what *you* think best. You go around running everyone's life, without regard for their wants or feelings."

His lordship began to pace the room. "I have a responsibility here," he said sternly. "I am doing my best to fulfill it."

Jocelyn could take no more. She, too, rose to her feet and advanced toward him, eyes flashing. "Your best, milord, is not very good. You are keeping my sister from the man she loves – a man with whom she could be very happy."

Ashburton turned to face her, his features set in angry lines. "How many times must I remind you that 'love' " – he said the word with obvious distaste – "is no criterion upon which to base a marriage."

"I suppose money is the proper criterion," Jocelyn snapped. "Can you men never think of anything else?"

Ashburton stopped again. "I assure you, Miss Franklin, I, at least, think of other things." That muscle beside his jaw twitched as though he were fighting to control some strong emotion. "But, in spite of your belief to the contrary, I have a sense of honor."

Jocelyn glared at him. "Honor! Really, milord! So now it is your *honor* that drives my sister to such misery!"

"I cannot expect you to understand!" he cried.

"Nor I you," stormed Jocelyn.

Ashburton scowled. "You persist in seeing everything I do in the worst possible light."

"Perhaps," returned Jocelyn crisply, "that is the best light in which to see it."

"Are you not aware," demanded his lordship, "that London is full of fortune hunters and that your sister is a prime target?"

"I am not a simpleton," snapped Jocelyn. "Of course I am aware. But Peter Ferris is not a fortune hunter, I know that."

"And I do not."

With great effort Jocelyn refrained from stamping her foot. How absolutely infuriating the man could be. "Have you no thought for Maria's feelings?" she cried. "What ever did you say to Peter Ferris?"

"I believe that is no concern of yours," returned his lordship angrily. "But, since I know your temper, I will tell you. I simply said to him that the Marchioness no longer needed his services."

"There was more to it than that?" Jocelyn demanded. "There must have been."

Ashburton stiffened. "I believe that I suggested to him that a man of honor would not offer for a woman that he could not properly care for."

"Oh!" For a moment, Jocelyn was speechless. "What a terrible thing to say to him. No wonder he left as he did."

His lordship smiled grimly. "So he has left. Good."

"What a perfect block you are!" cried Jocelyn. "The very fact that he left indicates that he is not what you suspect him of being."

Ashburton's scowl deepened. "He is gone. That's all I ask."

"And Maria is miserable. Haven't you seen her growing paler every day?"

The Viscount shrugged. "She will recover. 'Love' has never killed anyone."

"Perhaps not!" cried Jocelyn. "But it has certainly made a great number of people completely miserable." Her eyes filled with tears as she pronounced the words and she grew aware that she was speaking not just of Maria but of herself.

"My point exactly!" cried his lordship in triumph.

"Oh!" Jocelyn's hands clenched into fists as

she fought to control her rage. "It is not 'love' that is to blame," she said finally. "It's foolish people like you who make others miserable. When two people love each other –" Her throat seemed to close on the words. "They should be left to enjoy their happiness."

"All of this is very fine," cried Ashburton. "But it is still far from the point. What happiness could your sister expect in the hands of a penniless tutor?"

Jocelyn's nails dug into her palms. "They love each other," she replied. "They do not need a great deal of money."

"The Marchioness is worth a great deal," said Ashburton. "Peter Ferris is no fool. He knows her worth."

"I have told you and told you," Jocelyn returned. "Mr. Ferris is not after Maria's money. He loves her."

Ashburton drew closer to her and with difficulty she stopped herself from backing away. "Love is a delusion. So your heart beats faster and you long for someone's kiss. What does that signify?"

Jocelyn, conscious that her own heart was beating faster and that even in her anger she longed for his kiss, could not respond.

"It signifies nothing," answered his lordship. "No more than this."

While she watched with unbelieving eyes,

he reached out and pulled her into his arms. They were strong, lean, and hard, and she did not try to resist them. Struggle would be useless, she knew, and besides that, every fiber in her being longed for his touch.

As his head bent and his lips covered hers, Jocelyn felt a tide of emotion sweep over her. But this kiss was different from the others. Perhaps because she did not fight or resist it, it stirred a depth of feeling in her that even his previous kisses had not done.

For a long, long moment they stood thus, as his lips explored hers – tenderly, persuasively, with an insistence that frightened while it thrilled her. Then his lips left hers and moved across the curve of her throat to where a pulse throbbed.

He lifted his head slowly and stood looking down into her eyes. For a second she thought she saw a softening that might be love. But of course she was wrong. Ashburton would never feel such a thing.

"You see," he said softly, "something exists between you and me. Something that draws us to each other. We might dignify it with the name of love. We might even be so deluded as to base a marriage upon it. But surely any fool could see that such an alliance would be the biggest of errors." His eyes searched hers as though looking for something. "Would it not?" he asked, strangely intent.

She fought her way back to sanity. The most she could do was nod. There was no way to force any words past the lump that had formed in her throat. The realization hit her with sudden clarity that if it were not for Maria and Peter Ferris, she would throw herself boldly back into his arms and beg him to reconsider.

The thought of Maria made her realize that her nod could be interpreted in many ways. She forced herself to speak, though she could not meet his eyes. "The fact that you and I do not deal well together has nothing to do with Peter Ferris and Maria. Besides, the attraction – or whatever you wish to call it – that exists between us is not what Maria and Mr. Ferris have. Their devotion is based on respect. Can you understand that?" Her voice was low, but she managed to finish without a tremor or a break.

Ashburton's jaw, the strong line of which had softened as he looked into her eyes, hardened again. "I understand that Mr. Ferris would become a very rich man by an alliance with your sister."

"You could put the bulk of the estate in trust for Tom. Just give them an allowance to live on."

The Viscount laughed harshly. "The man

would never consent to that. I tell you, he wants control."

Jocelyn took a deep breath. "You are afraid," she accused, her head thrown back, "afraid that I am right. If you were not, you would do as I suggested."

Ashburton's scowl deepened. "You are the most impossible woman on the face of the earth."

"And you," cried Jocelyn, stung to the quick, "are the most impossible man!"

Chapter 17

Peter Ferris did return, just as Jocelyn had said he would. Just before the dinner hour he came back and closeted himself with a tearful Maria. Jocelyn, wishing she were there to help her sister, spent the time pacing the drawing room floor.

Finally, Maria appeared in the doorway. "Oh, Jocelyn, there you are. I must talk to you."

"Of course, Maria, I have been waiting. What is it?"

"You saw that Peter came back?"

"Yes? What did he have to say?"

"He has a new position, he says. He begins there shortly. The wage is not much, but we can live on it. I thought of my jewels, too. Oh, Jocelyn, may I leave them with you? Then I may get them as I need them."

"Of course, Maria. That is an excellent idea."

"Peter is speaking to his lordship now," Maria continued. "And then he will have the banns posted."

"Very good." For some reason Jocelyn could not feel the proper jubilation. Somehow, she felt Ashburton would foil this plan. Somehow he would stop them. She could not tell how, but he would.

However, she did not tell Maria this. "You are sure," she went on, "that you won't mind living simply?"

"Of course not!" Maria cried. "I never cared for all of this. I simply want to be Peter's wife."

"Then you shall be."

As Jocelyn accompanied her sister up the stairs to dress for dinner, she could not get rid of the feeling of impending disaster. She knew that Ashburton would not consent to Maria's alliance. Legally he could not stop her, but somehow, some way, he would manage. Jocelyn felt it in her bones.

And so, some five minutes later, when a

232

hurried knock sounded on her door, she was not surprised. She moved to open it.

"Oh, Jocelyn!" Maria was in tears again and Peter Ferris' face was stricken.

"He has beaten us," declared the tutor.

"Come in," said Jocelyn. "Tell me what has happened."

Peter Ferris guided the sobbing Maria to a divan and settled her there. Then the tutor turned to Jocelyn.

"Maria told you that I found a new position."

Jocelyn nodded.

"I went to his lordship to tell him that Maria and I intended to wed despite all he could do, that I had found a position and that I would care for her."

"Yes?" said Jocelyn, dreading whatever was coming next.

"He laughed at me." Peter Ferris clenched his fists. "He told me that I would never have Maria."

"But why?" cried Jocelyn, pushed past patience. "How can he stop you?"

Peter Ferris sighed. "He said that he would keep her children from her – that he would go to the Prince Regent, if necessary." The tutor seemed bent, as though under a heavy load. "There is no use in fighting any longer. I cannot compete with a man of such power. I have told Maria so. I cannot be responsible for the boys being separated from their mother. I must leave her. There is no other way."

Jocelyn, her knees going suddenly weak, sought for a chair and lowered herself into it. Her premonition had been correct. Ashburton would never allow this marriage.

Desperately she sought for something, some way out of this dilemma, but she could find none. She could only agree with the tutor.

Certainly none of them doubted that his lordship would act on his threat. The moment Maria became Peter Ferris' wife, her sons would be lost to her.

The tutor turned to the weeping Maria. "You know that I must go. And I must do it now, my dear. The longer I wait, the more painful it will be for the both of us."

Maria raised a tear-stained face. "No, Peter, you must not go. I cannot live –"

"Of course you can live," said Peter Ferris firmly. "We will both live – because we must."

"I shall never – never marry another," Maria declared, "no matter what his lordship says."

The tutor shook his head. "You must not make me any promises, my dear."

At these words Maria rose and threw herself into the tutor's arms. Jocelyn hurried from

234

the room and closed the door behind her. She rubbed blindly at her tear-filled eyes. There must be something, something that she could do.

She made her way down the staircase. She must see the Viscount; she must make him understand.

She paused outside the library door, wiping away the tears. This was a time to be strong. She knocked briskly.

"Come in." The sound of his voice threatened to bring on the tears again. Jocelyn swallowed hastily and pushed open the door.

"Miss Franklin," he said, "is there something I can help you with?"

His eyes were cold and distant and Jocelyn wondered bitterly how she could love such a man. She swallowed again in an effort to regain her composure. "I have just come from my sister and Mr. Ferris."

The Viscount's face darkened. "I supposed as much. But I assure you that no words of yours can sway me."

"But can't you see?" cried Jocelyn. "You have destroyed my sister's life. She will never marry now. She will spend the rest of her life alone."

"That is foolishness," said Ashburton sternly. "She will get over the man."

"How can you be so cruel? Can't you see

what you're doing?" Jocelyn knew that she was repeating herself, but she couldn't stop. Was there no way to make him understand?

"I believe that I have been very generous," he said. "I could have completely destroyed the man. One word from me and he would never be employed again."

"How very considerate you are!" snapped Jocelyn. "After destroying a man's life, you believe yourself generous because you have spared his livelihood and thus enabled him to live on in his misery."

"You are behaving far too tragically about this thing," he said with an attempt at lightness. "The delusion will fade. It always does."

Jocelyn's control failed her. "I hate you!" she cried in fury, flailing at him with clenched fists. "Oh, I wish I had never been born! Never seen you!"

At first, as her fists beat against his chest, he stood in startled surprise. But finally, realizing that she did not intend to stop, he pulled her against him and pinioned her arms to her sides. "Let me go, let me go!" she cried angrily.

But he simply held her there, crushed against his chest, until her anger had subsided into sobs. Gradually, she grew aware of a hand, tenderly caressing her back. "I am sorry to give you such pain," he murmured against her hair. "I am only doing what I must. If only you could trust me. But I know you cannot."

His words came to her softly, and for a moment she was not even sure that she had heard him. And then his closeness permeated her consciousness and she had to fight down her longing for him. But now she must. For now, even if by some miracle he should desire it, she could never, never be anything to him.

"You talk of trust," she said, pulling back and raising her eyes to his. "But you are not deserving of trust."

Ashburton shook his head, his eyes touched with regret. "I am sorry you believe that of me, but I can understand why."

Jocelyn found that she much preferred his anger to the look that he gave her, questioning her, entreating her understanding. "You do not understand anything about me," she said, drawing deep within for the strength to sustain herself. "And you never shall."

A sharp emotion passed over his features – pain, regret, bitterness – and then he straightened. "Of course. I should have know that you would never stoop to trust a man."

Now Jocelyn could feel her strength returning, coming back with the anger that his words inspired in her. "Perhaps," she cried, wrenching herself free from the arms that still held her, "perhaps that is because a man like you destroyed it!"

He winced as though she had struck him, and then he spoke formally: "As you wish, Miss Franklin. There is little point in my saying anything more." He swung on his heel and left the room.

Jocelyn, watching him go, felt her strength deserting her and sank to the divan in a heap. He had asked for her understanding and her trust, and she had denied him both. What else could she have done? She had no choice. Now he was gone, and she had sent him herself. For there had been an openness in his eyes, an appeal to her and a softness that could have been love. She knew it now, and it was too late. With a moan she dropped her head into her hands and let the tears flow.

Chapter 18

The next week was a miserable one. Maria moved as though in a daze. Her face blank of all expression, she greeted his lordship politely. She met several suitors, quite calmly rejected them, and quietly grew paler and thinner.

Jocelyn, fighting her own despair, was unable to offer Maria much comfort. There was certainly little hope that Ashburton would change his mind. The only thing left for Maria was to live for her sons, but even the boys had changed. Like frightened little mice they crept about the house, not making a sound, their usual cheerful faces drawn into sorrowful masks.

Through it all moved the Viscount Ashburton. He was seemingly unaffected by the havoc he had wrought. He was rarely seen, burying himself in work on the estate. When he appeared at meals his demeanor was perhaps more withdrawn, but he made polite, if stiff, conversation with anyone who addressed him, as though nothing around him had changed.

Jocelyn, for whom this behavior added insult to injury, said nothing. She did not trust herself to say a single word to him. Given the turmoil that raged inside her, there was no telling what might come out if once she began to give vent to her feelings. Alternately she hated everything about the man and then was filled by such pangs of longing for him that she felt physically ill.

So life in the house on St. James's Square went on its miserable way until one morning

Maria failed to appear for breakfast. Jocelyn, hurrying to her room, found her sister in a fever. "She is burning up," she declared to Rose. "Send immediately for a physician."

As the little maid scurried away, Jocelyn blinked back the tears. So it had come to this. Maria's constitution had never been of the strongest, and now, denied all hope, she had simply lost the will to live.

Jocelyn moved to dampen a cloth in the water pitcher and bathe her sister's fevered cheeks. As she did so, she talked. She knew that Maria could not hear her, but somehow it helped. "I'm sorry, Maria, truly I am. Perhaps if I hadn't antagonized him so. Or maybe I should have persuaded you to go to Gretna Green. He could not have undone it then. But I loved him; I hoped he would see, would recognize that we were right."

The tears slid down Jocelyn's cheeks and fell on her sister's burning face, but Maria did not notice them. Maria was deep in a delirium as she murmured, "Peter, Peter! Where are you?"

Jocelyn was filled with distress at seeing the agony on her sister's face. She felt that this whole terrible thing was her fault, and yet she did not know how she could have averted any of it.

When the doctor arrived some time later, Jocelyn was still at Maria's side, but nothing she did seemed to make her sister any more comfortable. Maria tossed and turned petulantly in the bed and every few minutes she called, "Peter! Peter! Where are you?"

Dr. Norris shook his white head and looked sorrowful. "She has brain fever. I'm afraid it doesn't look good."

Jocelyn felt her knees go weak.

"There's not a great deal you can do. We must bring the fever down – a cool bath, anything that works. Then we can only wait. Who is this Peter she calls for?"

Jocelyn was past caring about gossip. Her only thought was for her sister. "Her – She loves him."

"Then why isn't he here?" asked the old doctor irritably.

"The Viscount sent him away." Jocelyn could get no more words past the lump in her throat.

"Get him back," ordered the doctor. "Get him back right away or I won't answer for the consequences." He gathered up his bag. "I'll be back tomorrow. Shouldn't be any crises before then."

"Thank you, Doctor." Jocelyn, leaving Rose with the patient, followed Dr. Norris down the staircase. "Do you know – Can you tell me what caused it?"

The old man shrugged. "How has she been feeling lately?"

"She hasn't been eating much, nor sleeping, either, I suppose," Jocelyn replied, a catch in her voice. "She's been getting paler every day."

The doctor shrugged again. "That doesn't help. Even the strongest constitution can break under strain. Keep her as calm as you can. My advice to you is to get that Peter back here. That ought to help some. Then we'll just have to wait."

Then he was gone out the front door to his waiting carriage.

Jocelyn turned to Rears. "Have you any idea where Mr. Ferris' new position is?"

The old butler shook his head. "No, Miss, none. Is milady very ill?"

"Yes. We must find Mr. Ferris."

"But the Viscount has forbidden him entrance to the house."

Jocelyn's eyes grew icy. "I will answer to the Viscount. I do not intend to se Maria d—" Her voice broke on the word. "Send every footman. Scour London. Any man who finds Peter Ferris will have a reward. You, too."

The old butler looked pained. "There's no need for rewards, Miss. We all love her ladyship."

"Then find Peter Ferris and bring him here!"

"Yes, Miss. Don't you be worrying. We'll have him here quick as we can."

"Thank you." Jocelyn turned and hurried back up the stairs.

The day seemed to drag on interminably as Jocelyn continued to bathe Maria's feverish body and murmur soothing words to her.

The boys, creeping to the doorway with frightened faces, were given all the assurance she could muster. She could see that she had failed to comfort them and so offered them the only hope that she herself had left. "Mr. Ferris is coming. She'll be better then."

The childish faces brightened and Tom and Harold went quietly back to the schoolroom and the lessons they had been continuing on their own.

Jocelyn, turning back to her sister, could only regret again the mercenary dictates of a society that had separated these boys from the man they needed most.

But then Maria's fever rose higher and she tried to leave the bed. "I'm coming, Peter!" she called. "I'm coming!"

It took the combined strength of Jocelyn and Rose to keep Maria in place.

The sun was setting and Jocelyn had begun

243

to despair. Maybe Peter Ferris had left the city altogether. Maybe they would be unable to find him. And then she heard a bustle in the front hall. Dear God, it must be Peter! She sent Rose a glance and hurried from the room.

"You fool!" Ashburton's voice echoed through the hall. "This house is forbidden to you!"

"But, milord, I was –"

"There is no earthly reason for you to be in this house. Now begone."

Jocelyn gathered her skirt and hurried down the stairs. Peter Ferris' face was white. "I'm not too – late?"

"No. No. Mr. Ferris, you must go right up. Rose is there."

"Stop!" thundered Ashburton. "This man is not welcome here!"

For the first time Jocelyn turned her attention to the Viscount. He had evidently entered right after Mr. Ferris, whose hat and gloves she saw upon the table.

"You must listen to me," she said as Peter Ferris began to mount the stairs.

"Stop that man!" Ashburton thundered to the servants. But, though they all looked fearful and were obviously in awe of his lordship's power, to a man they stood their ground.

Ashburton took a step toward the stairs. "I

244

will stop him myself."

"No!" Without thought, Jocelyn threw herself at him and grabbed his arms. "You must not! Listen to me! Please!"

Never had she seen a face as thunderous as the one his lordship now presented. "Your silly ideas have gone too far," he said grimly, shaking himself loose of her grasp with such vehemence that she fell against the wall.

By the time she had recovered, he was halfway up the stairs. With a sob Jocelyn gathered her skirt and ran after him. She would stop him some way.

She ran through Maria's doorway and nearly collided with his lordship, who was just retreating. "You might have told me she was ill," he declared angrily. His eyes met hers, dark and devoid of emotion, his features set in harsh lines.

Jocelyn, her legs suddenly too weak to bear her weight, fell into a nearby chair and let the tears flow.

As she sat there she could hear the tutor's voice. Quite unabashedly, oblivious to her presence and that of Rose, he talked to Maria. Over and over he recalled to her pleasant memories of their days together. Over and over he reminded her that she had a duty to her sons.

Daylight faded and Rose moved quietly

about the room lighting candles, and still the quiet murmur of his voice continued.

Jocelyn, rising at last from her chair, sent Rose to rest and resumed the task of bathing Maria's face with cool water. Through the long night and into the next day she and Peter watched. She seemed to move in a timeless world that had no beginning or end.

Then, toward afternoon, Maria's plaintive cries became clearer. "Peter?"

"I am here, my dear. Right here. And I shall stay until you are well."

Maria's eyes opened. "Peter!" She reached out trembling arms to him and Jocelyn turned away. Such an intimate scene should have no onlookers.

Maria lapsed again into unconsciousness, but now Jocelyn had hope. Several hours later her sister again opened her eyes and this time she stayed conscious. Jocelyn bent to kiss her tenderly on the forehead. "Maria, my dear."

"Jocelyn," her sister murmured.

Jocelyn turned away, her eyes brimming with tears. She had almost conquered them, when she grew conscious of Peter Ferris standing beside her.

"I believe the fever has broken, Miss Franklin. Perhaps you should lie down a bit yourself now. Rose can send up another servant to relieve her, and I will remain, too."

"Thank you, Mr. Ferris." Jocelyn felt suddenly bone-weary. The shock of Maria's illness, the fear for her sister's life, and her confrontation with his lordship had all left her on the brink of exhaustion. "You must call me if she becomes feverish again," she insisted.

"Of course," the tutor agreed calmly. "But look at her. See how peacefully she sleeps?"

Jocelyn turned and could barely keep from bursting into tears of happiness. Maria was smiling gently in her sleep, her face peaceful. Without another word, Jocelyn stumbled from the room and made her way to her own chamber. Her eyes burned and every bone and muscle she possessed seemed to ache excruciatingly.

She fumbled at her gown and then, too exhausted to care, she collapsed on her bed fully clothed and fell into a deep slumber.

Chapter 19

The sun was streaming in the window when she awoke, and for a long moment Jocelyn could not recall why she had fallen asleep like this, with all her clothes on. Then she made a movement to rise and the stiffness in her body reminded her of the events of the day before. Dear God, Maria!

She sat up with a jolt, stifling a cry of pain as her muscles protested. She hurried from her room and down the hall to Maria's. Peter Ferris was seated by the bed, but one look at his relaxed face told her that all was well.

"Jocelyn," came Maria's voice from the bed, "oh, Jocelyn, I am so sorry to have caused you such trouble."

"You did not become ill on purpose," protested Jocelyn.

Maria smiled. "I know. But Mr. Ferris has persuaded me that I have acted foolishly. Neither of us considered that the boys must grow up, and when they do I shall be free. Mr. Ferris has promised to wait for me, Jocelyn. And I shall be good now and get better."

Jocelyn managed a smile, but she could not speak for the lump in her throat. It would be many long years before young Harold came of age. Yet somehow she could appreciate Maria's joy. If someday she could be assured of Ashburton's love –

The thought threatened to bring on new tears. But Mr. Ferris interrupted. "I do not know how much longer his lordship will permit me to stay. He looked in on us some time ago, but he said nothing."

"You must stay a while longer," insisted Jocelyn, her eyes on Maria's white hand that clung so tightly to the tutor's.

"As you say, Miss Franklin. It was really most kind of him to allow me to stay. We did not really give him much information."

"He did not stop yelling long enough to hear us," said Jocelyn with some rancor. But at least, once apprised of Maria's illness, he had the decency to leave the lovers alone.

She felt a sudden longing to see his face and turned toward the door. "I must get something to eat," she said, and that was the truth. She had eaten nothing the previous day. She had not even thought of it, but now her stomach was complaining of its ill treatment.

She would go first to her room and freshen up, she decided, but in the hall she was stopped by a footman. "His lordship said you were to have this."

Jocelyn took the proffered note. "Where is his lordship?"

"He left for his aunts' establishment early this morning, Miss."

"Left?"

"Yes, Miss. I have a note here, too, for her ladyship. He said I was to deliver them both together, so to speak."

"I see. Give me her ladyship's. I'll take it to her."

"Yes, Miss."

Jocelyn's heart pounded as she returned to Maria's room. Ashburton gone! What could it mean?

She hurried to the bedside. "His lordship has left us each a note. He has gone to his aunts'."

Jocelyn handed Maria her note, settled in a chair, and broke the seal on her own with trembling fingers. In great bold letters the words stood out: "YOU WIN." Nothing more.

There was silence in the room, and then came Maria's cry of happiness. "Dear God, he has relented! Peter! He has relented! We may call the banns when we please. He will keep the bulk of the estate in trust for Tom, but he will give me my usual allowance."

"Maria!"

As the two embraced, Jocelyn rose on trembling legs and left the room. She had won. Oh, yes, she had won. Maria and Mr. Ferris were guaranteed their happiness, but at what cost to her?

The man she loved hated her, hated her so much that he could not even bear to bid her farewell, so much that his last communication to her was a curt note.

Somehow she reached her own chamber and began blindly to throw things into her bags. She would leave London immediately. She felt an intense desire for the old house in Sussex, Perhaps there, where there were no memories of him to intrude, she could find peace.

The room was soon strewn with clothes, and Jocelyn knew that the sensible thing to do was to stop and call someone to help her. But she could not. She must get away from this house, from London, as soon as possible.

"Miss!" exclaimed Rose, coming upon the scene some few minutes later. "Whatever are you doing?"

"I'm packing. I must return to Sussex immediately. Please, Rose, send someone to help me and order my carriage out."

It was plain that Rose would like to protest further but didn't dare. Shaking her head, she made her way from the room.

In due course she returned with the information that the carriage would be ready shortly. "But surely, Miss, you could wait a day or so. You're apt to take sick yourself."

"No, no." Jocelyn frowned in a fever of impatience. "I must go today, as soon as possible."

"Milady is asking for you," said Rose.

"Of course. I'll go to her. Would you finish

this, Rose? I can't seem to make everything fit." She gestured toward the chaos of the room.

"Yes, Miss."

As she made her way down the hall, Jocelyn tried to compose herself. She must not let Maria see her in this condition. She put a smile on her face as she entered the room where Maria lay, with Peter Ferris by her side and the two boys, now smiling happily, playing with the pups in the corner.

"Jocelyn! What ever are you doing? Talking about leaving?" Maria's face was concerned.

"I must, dear. I have been here quite long enough. There are matters in Sussex that need my attention."

There was the sound of horses' hooves outside. "See, the doctor is here now. I'm sure of it."

"But, Jocelyn –"

"Please, Maria, I must." She turned away as her voice threatened to break. "I will write to you often. I promise. Now I must freshen up for the trip."

With tears blinding her eyes, she made her way back to the chamber that had been hers. "I've taken the liberty of laying out a fresh gown, Miss."

"Thank you, Rose. That'll be all."

"I'll stay and help you, Miss."

Jocelyn shook her head. "No, Rose, I want to be alone."

"Yes, Miss."

The little maid stood irresolute for a moment or two and then left the room, closing the door softly behind her.

Wearily, Jocelyn stripped off the crumpled gown and bathed her face and hands. She was still bone-weary, but she would sleep in the carriage. She would sleep more peacefully as the miles between them lengthened.

There came a soft tap on the door. Jocelyn sighed. "What is it now, Rose?" she asked as she began to dry her face.

There was the sound of the door opening and closing and footsteps crossing the room. Heavy footsteps. Jocelyn raised her head from the towel and her eyes widened in surprise. "Milord!" She clasped the towel over the front of her chemise.

The Viscount was already very close to her. He surveyed her evenly. "Where do you think you are going?" he demanded, his face devoid of expression as he looked down at her through dark lashes.

"I am going home. I am no longer needed her. I am going home to Sussex." She delivered this information to the front of his buff waistcoat, afraid to let herself meet his eyes.

"You have won," he said, an almost teasing quality to his voice. "Don't you want to crow over your victory?"

Jocelyn shook her head, her eyes still lowered, her voice husky. "You mistake me, milord. I do not wish to crow. Indeed, I wish to thank you for allowing my sister her happiness."

"You are quite welcome."

His tone was so strange that in spite of herself she raised questioning eyes to his.

"I *am* capable of recognizing a mistake when I have made one," he said ruefully, a half-smile on his lips, his eyes shadowed. "Conventions can sometimes blind us to the clearest truths."

Jocelyn nodded and looked away, unable to speak for the emotion that choked her.

"But why are you leaving now? Surely you will want to stay for the nuptials you worked so hard to bring about." His voice, though soft, was both demanding and persistent.

Jocelyn shook her head, drops of moisture still clinging to the tendrils of hair around her face. "No, no, I must get back to Sussex. I have been away too long." Still covering herself with the towel, she turned away from him, unable to bear his closeness and questioning any longer.

"What are you running away from?" asked

254

Ashburton, insistent.

Jocelyn stopped suddenly. There he went again. Always thinking he knew everything. She felt a surge of anger. Throwing the towel angrily to the floor, she spun on her heel to face him.

"I am not running from anything!" she cried hotly, color flaming in her cheeks. She strove to sound calm. "I am merely attending to my own affairs."

"Indeed!" His eyes were appreciative as they took in her figure, outlined by the clinging lace, her hair tumbling in confusion about her flushed face. She regretted the haste with which she had thrown away the towel, but she would not stoop to retrieve it. "I do not believe you," he continued.

"I do not *care* what you believe!" she cried wildly, turning away toward the bed.

Her shoulders were caught in a tight grip as he spun her around to face him. "I do not believe that, either." His eyes bore into hers. "You are running away from something."

Jocelyn felt the color flood her cheeks. "I am not!" She shouted the lie at him. "I am not!"

Suddenly his presence was too much for her. If she stood thus much longer, with his dark face so near her own, she would break and throw herself into his arms. And that was a disgrace she could not bear. She struggled to free herself from his grip, but he was too strong for her. He simply held her until she stopped fighting him.

"Let me go!" she cried desperately. "Haven't you done enough to make me miserable?" As soon as the words left her mouth, she realized her mistake.

"I?" He regarded her shrewdly. "Have *I* made you miserable?" His low voice was almost tender, the look he gave her intent.

Jocelyn grasped for straws. "Maria – Mr. Ferris. You kept them apart."

"But they are together now, are they not? I have seen the error of my ways." His grip did not loosen but had subtly changed, was almost a caress.

Jocelyn could only nod. She was fighting to control her body, which longed treacherously to throw itself into his lordship's arms.

"My responsibility for the Marchioness is over," he said, then looked at her consideringly. "But you still have no husband."

"Before God, but you are stupid!" Jocelyn knew she must get away from him soon. Perhaps if she could make him sufficiently angry. "Innumerable times I have told you. I have found no man whom I can l –" She swallowed over the lie. "Love and respect."

"I do not believe you," Ashburton repeated evenly.

"No!" Jocelyn shook her head vehemently. "There is no one. Nothing. No one."

"Then," he said smoothly, "you should be willing to consider an offer made for you."

Jocelyn looked at him with accusing eyes. "Milord! I want no husband."

"But this man wants you."

Jocelyn's mind raced in circles. Who could have offered for her?

"I'll refuse him."

His lordship frowned, his dark brows coming together, and shook her lightly. "Be sensible, you don't even know his name."

"It doesn't matter. I'll refuse him." Frantic to escape him, she struggled in his hands.

"And if he says he loves you?"

Jocelyn was on the edge of hysteria now. "It means nothing."

His grip on her arms tightened and he drew her toward him. She tried to twist away, her words incoherent, but her protests did no good. Inexorably, he drew her into his arms. She could not struggle; all her strength was gone. His mouth closed over hers, warm and demanding, by turns tender, then passionate, fierce, then gentle. It devastated her senses.

When finally he released her, she was half-blinded by tears. "You mock me, milord.

That is unkind." Her low voice faltered over the words.

"Unkind? And what of your behavior? You reject my proposal of marriage and dismiss my declarations. How else am I to convince you?" His grip tightened possessively.

"*Your* proposal of marriage?" she echoed, looking up at him with wide eyes.

"Yes, mine." He smiled wryly. "I thought that most courageous of me after you declared that you loved no one."

Jocelyn stared at him. Her heart thudded in her breast, her knees were weak, and she felt the blood flooding her already hot cheeks. "Marriage? You and I?" Her mind could not comprehend it.

"You and I," repeated Ashburton dryly. "I believe that is the proper procedure when a man and woman wish to share their lives." His eyes were half-teasing, half-tender.

"But – but we do not deal well together at all." Jocelyn could not believe what she was hearing; it seemed unreal.

"We did not get off to a very good start," he admitted. "I thought you were stubbornly thwarting all my plans to get your sister safely settled." He traced the line of her jaw.

"I was," she admitted sheepishly, looking down. "Really, milord. The way we fight! We shall be at cuffs constantly!"

258

The Viscount smoothed the hair from her forehead and said thoughtfully, "Perhaps. But consider. Our end was the same; it was merely in the means that we differed."

"But if we differ again?" asked Jocelyn, almost beginning to believe the feel of his arms around her, not wanting to question this idyllic moment, but unable to stop herself.

"Then we shall work it out. I am not always so obstinate as you have seen me." He kissed the tip of her nose. "You drove me to distraction, my love. So near and yet so distant. I was quite sure you detested me."

"But –" Jocelyn's face mirrored her confusion. "Why did you come back?"

"You gave your sister her happiness. She wanted you to have yours. She sent for me. I had come to inquire after her health and was about to leave when the footman found me."

Jocelyn put a hand to her fevered cheek. "But I told no one, not even Maria."

Ashburton's arms tightened around her. "She knew I might find it difficult to believe and told me how she discovered the truth. When she was ill, did you not talk to her?"

Jocelyn nodded. "Yes, but she was delirious when I talked about you."

"Unconscious people often hear what we say to them. She heard Peter Ferris."

Jocelyn could agree with that. "Milord, you

said –" She hesitated.

"I said that I love you." He spoke the words so tenderly that she felt her throat tighten. "I do." He smiled ruefully. "From the first day I saw you I was attracted to you. But I did not want to admit it. As for love – love was not an emotion that I recognized. You see, my aunts believed very strongly in discipline and brought me up with a very strong sense of right and wrong, duty and obligation. It is sometimes hard for me to see beyond their limitations." He smiled ruefully down at her and continued, half-apologetic. "I'm afraid much of my behavior was inspired by sheer jealousy, though I would not admit that at the time."

"Jealousy?" she queried, head to one side.

His hand curled into her hair, now tumbled down her back. "You were so beautiful, and so independent. I found your behavior – well, hard to accept." Jocelyn smiled impishly up at him. He returned the smile and continued.

"But no one else seemed to. Peter Ferris liked you. The Baron adored you. And you – you talked and laughed with them, never seeming to give me a thought. I was furious." His grip tightened unconsciously. "I'm afraid I was blind to Peter Ferris' good points because you so obviously liked him better than me." He raised a skeptical brow, as if daring her to challenge his statement, but she just smiled.

"Even when he offered for the marchioness, I could not view him dispassionately. And then there was the Baron."

Jocelyn giggled. "The Baron? How could anyone be jealous of the Baron?"

"He shared some of your interests; you could have managed him easily. And when he offered for you –"

"For *me?*" This time Jocelyn laughed aloud.

The Viscount looked at her sheepishly. "Yes, he did. I'm afraid I told him he was unsuitable. I told myself I knew you would refuse him and I was just sparing him the pain. But I knew it was because I was afraid you might not."

"Oh." Jocelyn smiled up into his eyes and traced his chin with a soft fingertip. "I would never have accepted the Baron, even if I hadn't loved you." She flushed and turned away.

He kissed her fingertips. "I was afraid to show my feelings for you, feelings I had never known before. I have experienced what it is to want a woman, but to love her – that is quite a different story."

"Those kisses." He took a deep breath, drawing her close to him. "You were so sure of yourself. You would not bow to my judgment or acknowledge that I was right. I suppose I wanted to prove my power over you. I do apologize. But in all fairness I cannot say I regret my actions." His eyes lingered on her lips.

"You were very unkind," she said, softening her words with a smile, "to treat me in that fashion."

"I know. But when you didn't respond as I expected, I was furious. I determined to show you." He laughed aloud. "I was not very successful, was I?"

Jocelyn laughed, too. "I cannot say, milord. It depends on what you wanted to show me."

"Well, in the end it was I who was at a loss. I was far more moved than I cared to admit and spent a great deal of time trying to convince myself that you were just another woman, easily forgotten – that I did not love you." He absently twisted a dark curl.

"Oh?" said Jocelyn softly.

"You were not forgotten." He kissed her gently on the forehead. "You did not make things at all easy for me, you know. I could not tell how you felt about me. At times you laughed at me. At times I felt you detested me. Sometimes I thought you cared, but I could never be sure. You really made matters most difficult." His dark eyes were warm as he looked down at her.

"I know," she said contritely, her eyes reflecting the warmth in his. "I am sorry about that."

"You will marry me, then?" he asked, his eyes searching her face.

"Oh, yes!" She smiled up at him and their lips met in a long and satisfying kiss.

After a while, the Viscount raised his head and looked down at Jocelyn consideringly. With a half-smile softening his autocratic features, he announced, "My solicitor will draw up the marriage agreement. I have decided that all of your property is to remain in your control."

Jocelyn gasped, a hand flying to her rosy cheek. "But, milord! Such a thing is practically unheard of!"

Ashburton shrugged. "Perhaps. The point is you have been managing it quite well previously, and you may as well do so in the future." He grinned at her, looking suddenly boyish. "That will give you less time to manage me."

"Milord!" Jocelyn protested, drawing back to chastise him, but unable to hide a pleased smile. She turned almost coquettishly and asked, "And what of love? Is it still a delusion?"

The Viscount Ashburton laughed. "I believe I made another error, mistaking for delusion what is, in sober fact, the ultimate reality. I assure you, my dear, I shall not make such a mistake again."